HARLEQUIN®
Presents~

The last, hazy days of August are meant for basking in the sun and reading good books. Whether you're relaxing in your backyard, on your porch or maybe chilling on vacation, make sure to have a selection of Harlequin Presents titles by your side. We've got eight great novels to choose from....

Bestselling author Lynne Graham presents her latest tale of a mistress who's forced to marry an Italian billionaire in *Mistress Bought and Paid For*. And Miranda Lee is as steamy as ever with her long-awaited romp, *Love-Slave to the Sheikh*, for our hot UNCUT miniseries.

You never know what goes on behind closed doors, and we have three very different stories about marriages to prove it: Anne Mather's sexy and emotional *Jack Riordan's Baby* will have your heart in your mouth while also tugging at its strings, while *Bought by Her Husband*, Sharon Kendrick's newest release, and Kate Walker's *The Antonakos Marriage* are two slices of Greek tycoon heaven with spicy twists!

If it's something more traditional you're after, we've plenty of choice: *By Royal Demand*, the first installment in Robyn Donald's new regal saga, THE ROYAL HOUSE OF ILLYRIA, won't disappoint. Or you might like to try *The Italian Millionaire's Virgin Wife* by Diana Hamilton and *His Very Personal Assistant* by Carole Mortimer— two shy, sensible, prim-and-proper women find themselves living lives they've never dreamed of when they attract two rich, arrogant and darkly handsome men!

Enjoy!

Sharon Kendrick

BOUGHT BY HER HUSBAND

Bedded by... 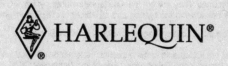 Blackmail
Forced to bed...then to wed?

HARLEQUIN®

TORONTO • NEW YORK • LONDON
AMSTERDAM • PARIS • SYDNEY • HAMBURG
STOCKHOLM • ATHENS • TOKYO • MILAN • MADRID
PRAGUE • WARSAW • BUDAPEST • AUCKLAND

ISBN-13: 978-0-373-12560-9
ISBN-10:   0-373-12560-7

BOUGHT BY HER HUSBAND

First North American Publication 2006.

Copyright © 2006 by Sharon Kendrick.

www.eHarlequin.com

Printed in U.S.A.

All about the author...
Sharon Kendrick

When I was told off as a child for making up stories, little did I know that one day I'd earn my living by writing them!

To the horror of my parents, I left school at sixteen and did a bewildering variety of jobs: a London DJ (in the now-trendy Primrose Hill!), a decorator and a singer. After that I became a cook, a photographer and, eventually, a nurse. I waitressed in the south of France and drove an ambulance in Australia. I saw lots of beautiful sights, but could never settle down. Everywhere I went I felt like a square peg—until one day I started writing again and then everything just fell into place.

Today I have the best job in the world: writing passionate romances for Harlequin. I like writing stories that are sexy and fast-paced, yet packed full of emotion; stories that readers will identify with and that will make them laugh and cry.

My interests are many and varied: chocolate, music, fresh flowers, bubble baths, films, cooking and trying to keep my home from looking as if someone's burgled it! Simple pleasures—you can't beat them!

I live in Winchester and regularly visit London and Paris. Oh, and I love hearing from my readers all over the world....so I think it's over to you!

With warmest wishes,

Sharon Kendrick
www.sharonkendrick.com

For the charming and talented Smith family...
Catriona, Steve, Lucie, Richard and Alice.
With love.

CHAPTER ONE

IN THE penthouse boardroom of the vast Christou shipping empire, Alexei Christou swung round in his chair and leaned back to gaze at the ceiling as the beautiful brunette who knelt before him began to unzip his trousers.

'Mmm,' he murmured. *'Omorfo.'*

A sigh of pleasure escaped from his lips, and he had just settled back to enjoy the ministrations of the ever-eager woman when the telephone began to ring. His mouth hardened with disbelief and fury and he tried ignoring it, thinking that the interruption might just go away. But it didn't go anywhere. Infuriatingly, it just rang and rang, and he snatched it up in anger.

'Ne? What the hell is going on?' he bit out. 'I told you that *under no circumstances* was I to be disturbed!'

He heard his male assistant give a nervous cough. 'Forgive me, Kyrios Christou, for making this one exception—but in the circumstances I thought—'

'What is it?' hissed Alexei, deadly as a snake.

'I have your...er...wife on the phone.'

There was a pause.

'My *wife*?' echoed Alexei softly, and the brunette jerked her head up from his lap to stare at him.

'*Ne, kyrios*. What would you like me to tell her?'

That she was a heartless, unfaithful bitch? That she was the biggest mistake he had ever made in his life and Alexei was not a man who tolerated mistakes in anyone—least of all himself?

His eyes narrowed. This was no doubt a follow-up call to the letter he had received from England—so it wasn't *completely* out of the blue. But even so, to hear from someone who had been out of your life for seven long years was a pretty strange sensation. Someone who had ripped through his heart and body and soul. A woman who had ensnared him and then betrayed him. His attention now fully engaged, he gave a cruel smile which would have filled his many business rivals with abject fear.

He held his hand up in a silent command for the brunette to stop what she was doing. Temporarily. It might not be the wisest thing in the world to be orgasming into her mouth while talking to his estranged wife—though in view of the way she had betrayed him might it not be a fitting revenge? His black eyes glittered. With ice for a heart—would she even care?

But Alexei resisted the temptation, recognising that such a self-indulgence would put him at a disadvantage—for what would it yield other than the momentary pleasure of release? There was a reason why men abstained from sex before battle and it was a good one. Sex weakened even the strongest of men, and Alexei was never weak—not any more. Not since the cheating witch he had married had disappeared from his life.

'Put her through,' he told his assistant softly.

In her poky London apartment, Victoria waited to be connected, clutching onto the telephone with a palm which was becoming clammier by the second. She was dreading this more than she could remember dreading anything—but maybe she would be immune to him by now. Immune to his potent sexuality and his unrealistic expectations of her as a woman and as a wife. Because she was not his wife, not any more—except in name—and even that wouldn't be for very much longer. She was no longer bound to him—she had been freed from the stifling prison of marriage to the formidable Greek. What Alexei thought was no longer her concern.

Just stick to the facts, she told herself as she stared at the pile of bills which just seemed to grow higher by the day. Tell him what you want as quickly as possible, and let that be an end to it.

And then at a last there was a click, and she heard a voice clip out one single, cold word. *'Ne?'* A familiar and threatening voice, and one which made the surface of her skin prickle and the beat of her heart begin to thump madly beneath her breast. Immune to him? As if.

'Hello, Alexei.'

Black eyes glittered at the sound of her soft English voice, but he kept his voice as neutral as if he were talking to any other enemy. 'Ah, so it *is* you,' he said tonelessly. 'What do you want?'

No, *Hello, how are you, Victoria?* Not even an attempt at social niceties—but what had she expected? Solicitous enquiries after her health from the man whose vicious parting words to her had been, *'You're nothing but a cheap, common tramp, and I rue the day I ever married you!'*?

'I…I need to talk you.'

'How fascinating,' he said, his voice deadly soft, like a tiger moving silently through the undergrowth towards its helpless and unknowing prey. 'About *what*, precisely?'

Victoria closed her eyes. The words of her lawyer came back to her.

'If you're after a swift settlement, I would be cautious in how you handle him, Mrs Christou.' And his even more disturbing follow-up. *'Your husband has the upper hand. Not because he's in the right, but because he's rich. Very rich.'*

He was right, of course. Rich men always won, because they could afford to employ lawyers to play long and obstructive games for them. And Alexei was richer than most. Millionaires were ten-a-penny in today's world, but Greek shipping billionaires did not exactly grow on olive trees. The last thing in the world she wanted was a protracted fight over money. Just as her lawyer had said...she must handle him carefully.

Victoria opened her eyes and stared hard out of the window at the grimy grey chimneypots of the London skyline. She was far enough away to pretend that she was talking into an answering machine, not to the charismatic Greek she had married.

Yet the simple words she had rehearsed over and over remained stubbornly stuck in her throat. Or was she simply reluctant to say them—knowing that once they had been uttered it really *would* be over? Because wasn't there a tiny part of every woman who wanted to hold on to their marriage—even if it had been a bad one? Everyone wanted to hang onto the fantasy, the dream of happy-ever-after.

'I...'

'Why, Victoria—you seem almost *nervous*.'

She could hear the cruel mockery in his voice. Keep cool, she told herself. 'Not exactly nervous,' she corrected him. 'More like apprehensive—and are you surprised? We haven't spoken in so long.'

'I know we haven't,' he said, stifling a moan—for the brunette was inching her fingers to where he had already been hard but was now harder still. He watched as the light gleamed on the scarlet of her fingernails and tried to shift the image of Victoria from his mind. Of her coming to him pure and untutored and him teaching her everything he knew about the art of love. He shuddered.

'Alexei?'

The voice at the other end of the phone broke into his confused thoughts and he groaned as he pushed the woman away. She sank back on her knees and stared up at him with a look of reproach, her scarlet lips shimmering as they folded into a faint pout. He shook his dark head and the pout intensified. But how could he have her do *that* to him when all her could think about was Victoria? Damn her! *Damn* her!

'Alexei?' Victoria frowned as she thought she heard him steady his breathing. 'Are you still there?'

'Ne.' He smiled at the brunette. The kind of smile which said, *When I'm finished with this damned phone call, then you can take me in your mouth and suck me dry.* 'But I am busy.'

So nothing had changed. Alexei Christou—a man with a mission and a tunnel vision which blinded him to everything other than making the Christou empire the biggest shipping company in the world. At least, that was what the papers said. Victoria had only seen his lust for power in its embryo stages— when it had devoured his life and excluded her, and begun the slow process of the disintegration of their marriage.

'What is it that you want?' said Alexei impatiently, giving a barely perceptible shake of his head as the brunette slid her fingers between her thighs and began to rub herself. *Wait,* he mouthed, and she pouted again.

'There are matters we need to discuss. Did you get the letter?'

'And what letter is that?' he enquired disingenuously. 'I receive many letters in the course of a working week. So many, in fact, that I can barely recall some of them. Refresh my memory for me, Victoria. What did it say?'

Don't let him intimidate you. You're no longer nineteen and madly in love with a dream. You're an independent businesswoman—even if you're not a terribly successful one. She gave a thin smile... understatement of the century.

'You know very well what it said. It was a letter from my lawyer,' she said flatly, 'telling you that I intend to file for divorce.' She took a deep breath. 'It's pointless ignoring it, Alexei—it isn't going to go away.'

'You want a divorce?' He gave a soft, taunting laugh. 'What makes you think I'll give you one?'

'*Give* me one?' she echoed. 'It isn't your *gift* to make! You don't have a choice!'

They had married young—Alexei had barely been out of college at the time, but his power and authority had grown in the intervening years. There were few people—in fact, not one—who would have dared to speak to him in such a way. His face darkened—and yet didn't he feel the delicious thrill of conflict? Wasn't there a tremor of excitement at the thought of doing battle—especially with *her*? For, deep down, didn't the corroding thought remain that he had never really *crushed* her—as she deserved to be crushed. The woman who had cuckolded him with another man!

'There is always a choice, Victoria *mou*. But what is this sudden rush? For seven years we have been apart, and you have shown no signs of wanting to be legally free of me. Why now? Have you decided to marry....?' He said something harsh in Greek which caused the brunette to look at him in shock. 'To marry your *lover*?' he finished in English—making the word sound as if it had nothing whatsoever to do with love. And it didn't. It was all to do with possession—and even now the thought of *his wife* having another man do to her the things he had once enjoyed filled him with a murderous rage.

'Is that why you want a divorce, Victoria? To please the man who has replaced me? Is it the same one you broke your marriage vows with? The one you took into your body before our marriage was a year old?'

Victoria swayed, a horribly familiar nausea clutching at her stomach—but she didn't bother trying to correct him. He wouldn't believe her if she told him that there was no replacement man waiting in the wings—as if anyone could replace *him*, even if there was! It was just another of Alexei's accusations and it was pointless trying to deny it. Her pleas of innocence had fallen on deaf ears in the past and always would.

He had painted a picture of her as unfaithful, and nothing would ever rid him of that image—no matter how far from the truth it was. Alexei saw the world as he wanted to. Maybe that was what all rich men did. He had a single-mindedness which was both his strength and his weakness, and nothing would ever sway him.

What had her lawyer said? *'Keep it short and keep it sweet—it's best that way. After seven years apart, there can't be a lot to say to say to each other.'*

Her lawyer, of course, did not know of Alexei's burning desire to always have the last word. To always be in the right. To get his own way, as he had spent his life doing. And—in spite of her intention not to do so—Victoria could not resist probing. But of course she was curious—what woman in her situation wouldn't be?

'You must be fairly keen to get divorced yourself, I would have thought?' she questioned innocently. 'I'm sure there must be a long line of women who are eager to become the next Kyria Christou?'

Of course there was! His cruel lips curved in anger. Did he mean so little to her that she could casually enquire about the women who had taken her place in his bed? The bitter seed of resentment, which had been planted so long ago and lain dormant for so many years, now began to spring into rampant and dangerous life.

Furiously, he acknowledged that she had somehow managed to kill his arousal stone-dead, and his fury grew. He waved the brunette away with an impatient hand and got up from his chair, going over to the window to stare out at the matchless blue of the Aegean sea, which was a sapphire stripe of ribbon in the distance.

'Naturally, I remain a magnificent marital prize in most women's eyes,' he boasted softly. 'But, unlike you, I have no desire to get divorced.' He saw the brunette turn around and stare at him reproachfully, and remembered that she knew more than a smattering of English. He pointed to the door and indicated five minutes with his fingers—softening his dismissal of her by blowing a kiss, and seeing her grudging smile in return. Some men might have felt guilty at such cavalier treatment of a woman, but not Alexei.

He never promised what he couldn't give—which was zero in the way of commitment. But he was never less than completely honest with the women who shared his bed, or who arrived on a whim to pleasure him when he was bored at work. From him they gained access to the most glittering parties around the globe. He bought them trinkets and jewels, and flew them around on his private jet.

Most importantly, he made them gasp with pleasure. Every single woman he had ever had sex with had told him that he was their greatest lover ever—and Alexei didn't doubt them for a moment. He prided himself on his sexual prowess—but to him it was yet another thing to excel at.

So what if the lovers in his life were foolish enough to believe that they would be the one to change his mind about settling down? Sometimes women only believed what they wanted to believe—which was nothing like the harsh reality. And that was not his problem. Either they faced the truth of what he could offer them—or they were history.

'You're saying you want to stay *married*?' Victoria was asking in disbelief as the penthouse door quietly closed and the brunette disappeared from his office with a final delectable wiggle of her lush bottom.

Alexei gave a humourless smile. 'That is not what I am saying at all,' he reprimanded softly. 'I said that I did not wish to get divorced—the two concepts are quite different.'

At that moment she hated him, and his clever, slick way with words—the way he could twist things round to make her sound completely stupid. And in a language which was not even his mother tongue!

'You're talking about interpretation,' she protested.

'We both know what I'm talking about, Victoria,' he retorted softly. 'I didn't get a lot from my marriage to you—but at least now it serves the purpose of keeping ambitious women off my back!'

Victoria bit back her outrage, knowing that Alexei's appalling attitude towards women had nothing to do with her—but her future *was*.

It was time to stop tiptoeing around his feelings. She had rights—and all she wanted was her freedom.

'Well, I *do* want a divorce,' she said coolly.

'Do you now?' He gave an exaggerated sigh. 'Then we seemed to have reached a sort of *impasse*.'

She heard the silken taunt in his voice and—despite all her vows not to let it—her temper flared.

'You can't stop me from getting one!'

'Can't I?'

There was a pause, and when Victoria spoke her voice was breathless. 'Are you…th-threatening me?'

'Threatening you?' He gave a low laugh. 'What a vivid imagination you have, Victoria.'

'Don't you *dare* patronise me!'

'Now, now.' His smile widened as he realised that he had very successfully hit his target. 'There is no need for hysteria.'

Which, of course, made her want to give in to exactly that. She could have *screamed*. Or told him that he was the most egotistical and controlling man she had ever met. But she forced herself to take a deep, steadying breath instead—because she needed all her wits about her if she wanted to challenge him on an equal footing. And why tell him something he already knew but didn't particularly care about?

'Do you want me to have the papers served on you, Alexei? Because you're going the right way about it!'

He gave another low laugh of pleasure as he heard the fury in her voice. How could he have forgotten how stimulating resistance could be? He might have a whole list of complaints about the woman he had been misguided enough to marry—but boredom had never featured on it. 'You'd have to find me first,' he challenged.

'Oh, that's possible—believe me. My lawyer can engage someone in Athens to track you down and serve you with divorce papers. This kind of thing happens all the time, you know—errant husbands refusing to face up to their responsibilities!' And suddenly she stopped, aware that she had said too much.

Alexei drew in a silent and thoughtful breath. It sounded as if she had done her research. And it sounded as if she wanted money. His eyes narrowed. How much of a claim on his fortune was she intending to make? he wondered. He ran a speculative finger over the shadowed rasp of his jaw, which had

sprung up despite an early-morning shave grabbed
on the run from the brunette, who seemed to have
discovered the principle of non-stop pleasure and
was eager to put it to the test.

He stared out to sea, where he could see a ship
moving slowly along the blue horizon—a Christou
ship. It was just one of a mighty fleet of vessels
which were renowned the world over and owned
exclusively by the Christou family—with Alexei as
its figurehead. Shipping brought untold wealth, and
Christou dominated the market.

Could he be bothered even to fight this divorce?
Alexei stretched his arms above his head and
yawned. Even a weighty claim by most people's
standards wouldn't even make a dent in the Christou
billions. Shouldn't he just sign Victoria her cheque
and wave goodbye?

But his heart began to thud rhythmically in his
chest.

Damn it, yes! He *would* fight her—as she deserved to be fought—for she had hurt and betrayed
him. She had let him down, and that had been a
hard lesson for a man like him to learn. He had held
her in the kind of regard and esteem that he had felt
for no other woman, and what had she done but hurl
it all back in his face?

And in a way hadn't he been expecting this for a
long time? His estranged wife had surprised him by
not demanding a slice of his fabulous wealth within

months of the marriage ending. And then months had become years. It had become a stand-off, and he'd known that one of them would have to break it—but he had also known that it would never be *him*, for his fierce pride would not allow it. It had been a long, long wait, but it seemed that the time was here at last. And he meant to enjoy every second of it.

'Even if you manage to serve me with papers,' he said softly, 'it doesn't mean that I'll co-operate with you.'

Victoria bit her lip. This was the worst-case scenario her lawyer had warned her about. He could play tricks with her and eke it out, and although she would win in the end it could take months, even years. In the meantime her debts would be mounting, with interest accruing—and with a business as small as Victoria's just one large, unpaid bill could be enough to throw the whole thing out of kilter.

But it was more than the money she now owed as a consequence of that. Much worse was the knock-on effect on the woman who worked for her and relied on her. She knew Caroline's circumstances and they weren't easy. She had worked her socks off and shown Victoria nothing but loyalty— and Victoria was not prepared to jeopardise that dear woman's livelihood on the say-so of her arrogant ex.

'So you want a fight, Alexei, do you?'

'Fighting is in my blood,' he murmured. 'You know that, Victoria.'

But he had never fought to keep her, had he? He had given up on her at the earliest opportunity—willing to believe the very worst of her. And a battle was the last thing she wanted or needed with a man who still had the ability to make her heart race—though today that was surely more through anger and frustration than instant turn-on?

Victoria looped a lock of hair behind her ear. *Just take emotion out of the equation,* she urged herself. *Talk to him as if he's a client just about to choose the menu for the tennis club's annual dinner. Don't let him realise he's getting to you.* 'Is there nothing which will make you change your mind and reach a peaceful solution?' she asked calmly.

Despite the suddenly reasonable tone she had adopted—Alexei recognised that this was the key question—and that with it she had just handed him the baton of power. A small smile curved his lips as he enjoyed the familiar feeling of being in control. And what better feeling could there be other than orgasm itself? But control lasted much longer…

Staring out at the azure sky, he anticipated the simple fish he would eat for lunch beneath a flower-decked canopy in a hidden green oasis of the city. Perhaps afterwards he would take one of his yachts out. Have a massuese on board, and maybe the brunette, too. He yawned. If he still had a hunger for her.

'Perhaps there is,' he said silkily, and he paused deliberately, because he knew that silence on the telephone could sound like an eternity to an adversary. 'Why not come out here and we'll discuss it?'

Victoria stilled, every instinct in her body shrieking its alarm as she listened to his suggestion in disbelief. 'To...to Athens, you mean?'

'Why not?'

'Don't be so ridiculous, Alexei!'

'You think it such a bizarre suggestion?' he mused. 'Yet it is where I live and where you once lived—the place you once called your home, though we both know what a myth *that* was. For your life here was as much of a sham as your supposed desire to be a good wife. Is that why you cannot face Greece again, Victoria?'

She could think of plenty of reasons—but Alexei was the main one. The last time she had seen him he had told her that he would sooner go to hell than ever set eyes on her again. So what had changed? Instinctively Victoria licked at lips which had grown dry. Nothing had changed—for weren't the insults still flowing thick and fast? He hated her—and he was making that very plain.

'I can't see the point,' she whispered.

'Can't you? Maybe I might be a little more...

considerate if you came and asked me to my face for a divorce.'

'*Ask* you?' she echoed, but her heart had now started thumping nervously in her chest. 'You think I need to ask your *permission*? That I need your consent? We aren't living in the Dark Ages!'

But in a way Alexei was—and he always had been—it was just that Victoria had been too young to see it at the time. For all his modern American education, beneath the exquisite Italian suits and handmade shoes there beat the heart of a primitive man.

'This is all about the law, Alexei—and you don't make it! Not in England, anyway!'

'But I am a Greek,' he reminded her proudly. 'And you are married to a Greek.'

She opened her mouth to tell him that that didn't matter. But she bit back her words. She had already said more than enough. He would know she had been doing her legal homework, and that would make him an even tougher adversary. But Alexei had spoken the truth—he *was* a natural fighter. Surely there was another way around this?

Surely they could draw a line under their mismatched marriage and wish each other well for the future? So that, even if the idea of being friends was an unrealistic one, at least they could have each other's best interests at heart. And you would not wish harm to befall someone whom you had once loved to distraction, surely?

'Come and see me,' he said softly, his voice cutting into her thoughts. 'Or maybe you don't dare to, Victoria?'

Did she?

Once she had been like a piece of soft toffee in his experienced fingers. He had warmed her with his expert caress and the silken touch of his tongue. One sensual look from Alexei had been enough to reduce her to a melting state of desire.

But seven years was a long time, and she had grown from girl to woman. A woman who had more sense than to fall head-over-heels a second time for a black-eyed devil who knew how to send a woman to paradise and back with his body.

But not how to love her or trust her or properly share his life with her.

'If I agreed to a meeting, then couldn't it be here—in London?' she added hopefully. That would be much better. They could meet in some anonymous hotel in the centre of the city and then afterwards she could hop on a bus and leave his life for ever.

Alexei smiled as he anticipated that he was about to get exactly what he wanted. Outside, the heat from the blistering sun frazzled off the buildings, though inside the air was as cool as spring water. He loved this capital city, despite its noise and its heat and its chaos, for it pulsated with life and colour and vibrancy. And it would amuse him to see his cool, English wife here once more—who in her way was the city's very antithesis. Would he still desire her? he wondered idly.

'I'm not planning to come to London,' he said carelessly.

'But it's...easier for you to travel here.'

His sensual mouth curved into a predatory smile as he heard her diffident tone, and like a hungry vulture who had spotted a fragment of fresh flesh glistening on a dusty road he pounced on her sudden uncertainty.

'And why is that, *agape mou*?'

The term of endearment made her face colour painfully, but the cynical way he said it allowed her to close her mind to the memories it provoked. 'Because your job is...flexible,' she said, hating herself for faltering—but how could she just come right out and say, *Because you're filthy rich and can do as you please, and I have to work for a living. Because I have a pile of ceiling-high debts and I'm not even sure I can afford the airfare out to Greece*?

He smiled with heartless delight. 'That, of course, is the beauty of being your own boss,' he observed.

'Well, I'm my own boss, too!' she retorted, stung. 'And—unlike you—I didn't have it handed to me on a plate.'

His eyes narrowed, for he was never criticised.

'Just what type of work *are* you doing these days, Victoria?'

She stared at the sugar fondant roses which were lying on the work surface, ready to garnish a birthday cake she'd just made. Although they were dusted white with sugar, beneath that they were still pink—like the bouquet she had carried on her own wedding day. It didn't matter that the marriage hadn't lasted, or that she had schooled herself into pushing it into the recesses of her mind—because deep down it still existed. She couldn't completely wipe it away. And sometimes the memory could twang away mercilessly at her heartstrings and make her want to yelp aloud with self-pity.

But self-pity was a most unattractive emotion, and it never got you anywhere.

'I'm still in catering, Alexei,' she said crisply. 'Nothing's changed.'

'Then I suggest you take a break from your catering.'

'I'm not with you.'

'Come to Athens and we will thrash out a settlement between us,' he continued remorselessly. 'Because if you want a divorce that's the only way you're going to get one.'

He put the phone down and issued a short, terse command into the intercom. The door opened and the brunette returned, unbuttoning her dress as she walked slowly across the office towards him.

CHAPTER TWO

'VICTORIA—do you really think this is wise? You don't have to go crawling to your ex-husband, you know! And certainly not for *my* sake!'

Caroline's voice was vehement, and Victoria paused in her packing to look at her oldest friend. They'd met years ago at college, but Caroline had been forced to drop out early when she became pregnant.

Victoria had provided a shoulder to cry on when the baby's father had done a runner, and had sat with her friend during a long labour as her birthing buddy.

And Caroline had been there to return the favour when Victoria's marriage broke down and she'd barely been able to bring herself to get out of bed in the mornings. On good days they'd used to joke that they had both packed in some pretty heavy life experiences very early on. On bad days they hadn't joked at all.

When Victoria's catering company had begun to do well, she'd realised that she was going to need help—and her old friend had been the perfect answer. As a single mum, Caroline was glad of the work and of a flexible boss—and she was a talented cook. Thus a temporary arrangement had become a very happy permanent one.

Victoria folded a T-shirt and put it in the bag. 'Point one—I'm not crawling to *anyone*. I'm entitled to some kind of settlement, and I owe it to myself to get it,' she said slowly. 'And point two—I'm not doing it for your sake. That sounds like I'm doing you a favour, and I'm not. My company owes you the money and I'm damned well going to make sure you get it. And let's face it,' she added gently, 'you've got rent to pay and a child to look after.'

Caroline looked anxious. 'I can't bear to see you looking as worried as you've been this past week. Honestly—I can manage somehow.'

'You shouldn't have to.' Victoria closed the small bag. 'Anyway, this goes much deeper than a debt. This is something which is long overdue. I can't carry on pretending the marriage never happened—that it will go away by itself. I need some sense of closure.' She sighed. 'I've been a coward where confronting Alexei is concerned.'

'I'm not surprised. He was a pig to you—I can't understand why you married him in the first place.' Caroline pulled a face. 'Well, maybe I can!'

Their eyes met in an unspoken moment of ac-knowledgement of why she *had* married him.

What woman in the world wouldn't have been

bowled over by Alexei Christou if he'd made up his mind that he wanted you?

Now it was easy for Victoria to step back and see that she'd been completely out of her depth—but no one could stop themselves from falling in love. She hadn't been the first naïve young girl to do it, and she wouldn't be the last—only in most cases it would have just been a short, passionate affair instead of a foolhardy marriage.

'He's just—'

'Spoiled!'

'Well, maybe—if spoiled means having been given everything you wanted all your life, which of course he has.' But *spoiled* made him sound like a little boy—and if there was one thing that Alexei was, it was all man. Very definitely. She shuddered. 'He's just operates in a different league, that's all. His life is nothing like mine—and it's about time I was free of him.'

'But you are!'

Victoria shook her head so that her silky mane of blonde hair caught the light and shimmered. 'That's just it—I'm not—not really. As long as I remain married—even if it's only in name—then I remain tied to him. And that's hopeless. I have to move on,' she said, but she was aware that just speaking to him again had stirred up all kinds of troubled emotions.

Caroline handed her a tube of suncream. 'How do

you feel about seeing him again?' she asked suddenly.

'I'm dreading it,' said Victoria truthfully.

She felt churned-up as she boarded a Greece-bound flight on a budget airline and settled herself back into her cramped seat—thinking how differently she had travelled to Greece in the past.

This time around she was surrounded by young backpackers who were happy to purchase their own sandwiches and drinks from the aircrew who wheeled trolleys up the narrow aisle. Yet when she'd been married to Alexei they had flown in style. And what style! The first time he'd taken her to his homeland Victoria hadn't quite believed what was happening to her. It had been like stepping onto the set of a film—the kind of Hollywood blockbuster where the director had said there was no limit on the budget.

One of the Christou family jets had been made available to them, along with its own fleet of glossy crew. But even in the midst of her personal happiness at having married the man she had fallen in love with Victoria had begun to feel the first goosebumps of foreboding. An outsider. An English girl. And poor, to boot. The gorgeous stewardesses had given her barely-concealed looks of amazement. As if to say—Why the hell has he married *her*?

She remembered thinking the same thing herself.

Self-consciously she had smoothed down the skirt of the brand-new dress Alexei had bought for her, remembering what her mother had said—*Fine feathers make a fine bird*. Did they? Did she look good enough for her Greek billionaire?

Perceptively, he had tilted her chin to look at him, the black eyes narrowing and bathing her in their ebony light. 'My wealth—it intimidates you a little, *agape mou*?' he had asked softly.

Some of his vigour had flowed to her through his fingertips, and Victoria had suddenly felt as strong as he was. 'I don't give a stuff about your wealth!' she'd declared passionately. 'I would love you if you didn't have a drachma to your name!'

He had looked at her with purring approval, but maybe Victoria would have done herself a favour if she'd confided to him that the people who surrounded him *did* intimidate her. That it wasn't easy when everyone was wondering what your new husband saw in you and how long it would last. And if he had known—might it have changed things?

Victoria viciously snapped off the ringpull from a can of cola and drank from it thirstily. *Stop it,* she told herself. Don't remember times like those. Remember the reality. Which was hell. You're going to Athens with one objective in mind. To see Alexei and to draw a line underneath the marriage. And he has forced this situation on you. He's as controlling as he ever was—so remember *that*, too.

She stared out of the window as the plane flew over the impossibly blue Aegean sea and then began to descend on the high looming clutter of buildings which was Athens itself. As the ground rose up to greet them she could see the crazy architecture and the congested traffic on the streets below. Everyone had a view of Athens as noisy and hot and dusty. But Victoria knew of another city—a secret Athens—one which had been shown to her by Alexei and one tourists were seldom privvy to.

He had opened her wondering eyes to the small green parks hidden away from the busy life of the main drag. She had eaten in lively little family-run tavernas which were lit at night by strings of coloured lights looped through the trees, while people danced as if they had fire in their veins and beckoned for you to join them. And there had been Alexei—barefoot and dancing, too—his black head thrown back in laughter.

Despite her determination not to indulge in sentimentality or nostalgia, she felt a pang of regret as the plane touched down in his homeland. In England it had been simpler to try and put him into the darkest recesses of her mind and to think of the whole experience of her marriage as another faraway life she had once lived. But she was going to have to accept that this trip was bound to throw up painful reminders of all that he had meant to her.

She had just better be prepared for it—forewarned

meant forearmed—and instinct told her that she was going to need all her wits about her. If she weakened—allowed misplaced emotion to make her vulnerable—then she would be easy prey for her clever, calculating husband.

Picking up her overnight bag, Victoria went outside to where the heat was bouncing off the tarmac and beating down on her pale skin—even though it was only June. Her skin was sheened with sweat as she climbed into the back of a yellow cab, and her cotton dress just beginning to stick to her body, but thankfully the taxi was air-conditioned, and she leant back on the seat with a sigh of relief.

The radio was blaring, the driver was singing, and worry-beads were swinging from the mirror with a little clatter. Outside, the traffic was bumper-to-bumper, but the sky was blue, and unwillingly Victoria remembered that this was the home of the Parthenon and the Acropolis, that this was where legend said the goddess Athena had invented the olive tree.

And she found herself wishing she were just an ordinary tourist—geared up to having a fabulous holiday in the sun—instead of going cap in hand to her wealthy ex.

It was stop-start most of the way, until the taxi stopped outside the impressive steel and glass tower of the Christou headquarters. Nervously, she over-tipped the driver, and could feel the palms of her hands growing clammy as she stepped inside the revolving doors which delivered her into a space-age foyer.

The air-conditioning hit her like an ice-cube. Tiny goosebumps began to appear on Victoria's arms as the sleek brunette at Reception stared at her as if she had just landed from Mars.

The woman rattled off a question in Greek and then, as Victoria frowningly attempted to translate, she spoke again—this time in perfect fluent English.

'Can I help you?' she questioned, in a tone of voice which suggested that Victoria might be in the wrong building.

'I'm here to see Kyrios Christou,' said Victoria.

'Kyrios *Christou*?'

'*Ne,*' agreed Victoria, dredging up a word in Greek from its dusty memory bank.

'What is your name, please?'

'It's Victoria.' She forced herself to smile at the unfriendly face. 'Victoria Christou.'

Was it only her well-travelled appearance which made the brunette's mouth fall open into a disbelieving 'O'? Victoria wondered.

'Christou?' the woman repeated blankly.

'Yes.' Victoria nodded enthusiastically, seizing on the unexpectedly enjoyable moment—because she certainly wasn't anticipating a lot of *those* during her visit. 'I'm his wife. I believe he's expecting me—though I didn't give a precise time. You know what scheduled flights are like!'

'He is *expecting* you?' said the brunette again.

And suddenly Victoria's social attennae were alerted to the fact that this response would hardly win prizes for professionalism. So was the woman just having an off-day, or did Alexei discourage callers by employing this rather attractive dragon to ward them off?

Unlike the brunette, she wasn't wearing a designer linen dress—though how she could afford it on *her* salary, Victoria didn't know—but surely she didn't look *that* bad?

'Perhaps you could just let him know I'm here?' asked Victoria coolly.

The brunette laughed briefly, as if someone had just given her a piece of exceptionally good news. 'It will be my pleasure,' she said, as she picked up the phone and spoke rapidly into it, but the smile disappeared from her face when she was obviously given instructions to send Victoria straight up.

It was during the elevator ride that Victoria's nerves came back to assail her—not helped by a peek at what she actually looked like. Unfortunately—or maybe that should have been fortunately—the lift was mirror-lined, which allowed her to see just how the journey had taken its toll. Perhaps the brunette's incredulous reaction was understandable, after all. She tried telling herself that she wasn't trying to wow Alexei, but even so there was a proud side to every woman who wanted her ex to still think she was drop-dead gorgeous.

Pulling a plastic pack of wipes from her handbag, she removed some of the grime from her face. Her hair was tied back, but she brushed out her fringe just as the lift pinged to a halt. No time for lipstick.

Oh, well.

A male assistant was waiting to greet her, and she followed him through a series of increasingly grand offices until finally he opened the door to one where a still, dark figure was standing with his back to her. Was that deliberate? she wondered. Of course it was!

He was looking out over the backdrop of Athens, and Victoria's heart lurched as she saw the man she had once adored as much as life itself. The man who had taken her virginity. Who had told her he loved her and then shown her that love could break your heart. The man she'd married.

Alexei Christou.

Though the huge plate-glass windows were faintly tinted, the light still gleamed on his ebony-dark hair—worn just a fraction too long—so that instead of an heir to a billionaire shipping fortune he looked more like a sexy bandit. Or a very fit pool man... A rich woman's fantasy lover.

And a poor one's, too.

Victoria froze as he slowly turned his head, praying that her face and body were registering nothing other than...

What?

That was the trouble—what were the rules in a situation like this? How did you behave and react towards a man you hadn't seen for seven years to whom you'd once been married? This was the man who had symbolised all her romantic hopes and dreams—and then had come to symbolise her own sense of failure and regret.

For Alexei had left his own dark legacy in her life—creating an impossible act for another man to follow. It didn't seem to matter if a man had stepped out of the 'suitable partner' section at Central Casting—when compared to Alexei Christou they all seemed as two-dimensional as a cardboard cut-out.

Even now he had the power to throw her into a state of confusion. If only she could be sure of her true feelings towards him—because surely it would be easier if she hated him. But as she stared at him across the expanse of the room it wasn't hate she was feeling. Far from it. She was smacked sideways by a sensation she most definitely did *not* want to experience.

Was it desire which made the blood begin to roar in her ears and her heart begin to leap and race beneath her breast? She felt dizzy. As if her body didn't belong to her any more. It was like looking down the wrong end of a telescope—her world had reduced down to just the space of one face. His face.

And, oh, it was impossible not to drink in all its hard and arrogant beauty. The luminous olive skin and the lush mouth, with its curved and slightly full lower lip. Lips which had kissed every single bit of her body and taken her to paradise over and over again.

But it was the eyes that drew her in, more than the memory of those sensual pleasures. Black and glittering, they had once stared at her with love— but now they studied her with nothing more than contempt, their cold ebony light raking over her.

Her heart-rate only increased. How could it not? She could feel it crashing loudly against her ribs and was surprised he couldn't hear it.

Alexei, she mouthed, though no sound came from her lips, and suddenly she was having difficulty focussing.

Her vision blurred and then became clear again— and her head spun as her mind wickedly played tricks on her, dragging her back into that painful place she had vowed never to visit again.

But sometimes you had no choice, because the past had a pulling power all of its own.

CHAPTER THREE

WHEN Alexei had first blazed into Victoria's life she'd been just nineteen—an ordinary catering student living on a stingy grant, taking extra jobs whenever she could. When many girls her age had been out partying, she'd found herself putting prawns into hundreds of little pastry cases. Or sprinkling glistening little black caviar eggs onto smoked salmon—if it was a particularly upmarket party.

Very occasionally she'd be required as 'front of house', as a waitress—expected to tie her hair back and don a smart uniform, and waft around glorious rooms offering trays of canapés to the great and the good and the extremely rich.

The night she'd met Alexei she'd had no idea what the party was for or who the guests were. It had been just another function in a golden ballroom in a glorious house overlooking St James's Park. The central London location had been as fancy as you could find—and the guests had more than done it justice. There'd been lots of thin women wearing some serious jewellery, and very loud men who'd given a whole new meaning to the word 'lecherous'.

Victoria had been so busy handing out champagne

and blocking murmured innuendoes that she hadn't even noticed the exotic-looking man with the exceptionally dark hair on the other side of the room.

Alexei had been bored. He'd been at the tail-end of a globe-trotting trip which was a reward from his father for his first-class degree from Harvard. He had recently travelled to Paris, Milan and Madrid—as well as Prague and Berlin. The achingly familiar taste of Europe had reminded him just how much he had missed it, but he couldn't wait to get home. To Greece.

He hadn't been sure at just what point the waitress had imprinted herself on his consciousness and set in motion all the complex factors which determined desire and sexual chemistry. She wasn't particularly to his taste—she was fair, when he liked his women dark—but she'd moved with exquisite grace, despite the faintly old-fashioned silhouette of her hour-glass figure.

He'd watched her weaving her way in and out of the crowd, the way she'd managed to make the commonplace movement of offering a tray into some intricate, music-less dance. And the fact that every man in the room must want her—had that fuelled his determination to have her—he who could always have the pick of any woman he chose?

Come here, he'd willed her. And—as had happened during so much of a life which many called charmed—she'd chosen just that moment to obey his silent command.

Had the intent gaze fixed so unwaveringly in her direction made Victoria look up to find herself imprisoned in an enchanting ebony blaze? Had it been his height or his very *foreignness* which had made her own glance linger for a fraction longer than entirely necessary?

And she'd found herself blushing—stupidly and infuriatingly *blushing*. As if no man had ever looked at her like that.

Because no one had. Well, certainly not a man like that—not in a way which had made the breath catch in her throat and her stomach curl into a warm mush of pleasure.

But she'd deliberately turned away—and that had been the necessary reaction to him. Because Victoria had long ago accepted the unrealistically romantic side to her nature, which she reined in as if it were a dangerous animal for fear of what havoc it could cause were it released.

For Alexei, the back turned on him—with the fold of fair hair pleated against a long, slender neck—had been tantalising. The very gesture of rejection had been as appealing as the woman herself. Later—much later—he would reflect on the significance of this, but for now his hormones were raging around his bloodstream in a torrent of longing.

He had waited for her to come to him—as come

she must. Not simply because she was there to provide a service for the hosts, but because he had compelled her to do so. And it was working. It always
worked.

Her face had been flushed and almost defiant as
she'd drawn near.

'At last,' he murmured.

'Canapé, sir?'

He waved he plate away impatiently. 'What time
do you finish?'

'That's a very impertinent question, sir.'

'I'm a very impertinent man,' he breathed, and
smiled a smile which would have been perfectly at
home on the face of one of his forebears—those
gods of myth and legend. 'If I promise to behave
like a…gentleman—' his black eyes mocked her
'—and to deliver you home before the break of
dawn, will that make a difference?'

Victoria hesitated, sensing he was trouble, and
yet…

'Nine o'clock,' she said crisply. And she turned
and walked away, telling herself that he wouldn't
bother turning up and that it was probably a party
game he played to pass the time—seeing how many
women would agree to meet him.

But he was waiting for her at the staff entrance,
looking sombre and yet enticingly dependable in a
dark overcoat with its collar turned up against the
unseasonably chill wind.

'Shall we eat something?' he questioned. 'Or does working with food spoil your enjoyment of it?'

It was a perceptive question, which naturally only added to his appeal. 'Sometimes. But I'm not hungry,' she said.

'Me neither.' Well, not for food. But you couldn't tell a woman whose name you didn't even know that the only thing you wanted to eat was *her*.

It had none of the ingredients for a suitable romance—certainly not from Alexei's point of view. She was English, and poor, and not particularly well educated. On the plus side she was very beautiful—and still a virgin. But that incredulous discovery carried with it the burden of responsibility. To his astonishment and annoyance, he discovered a nagging conscience—realising that he could not simply bed her and then abandon her! In fact, she had none of the qualities he was looking for in a partner—and he wasn't even *looking* for a partner!

But Alexei was failing to take into account something he hadn't thought could happen to him—for emotion wasn't high on his list of priorities. And when it did finally happen, he didn't recognise it. He tried to deny it. Until his denials sounded hollow—even to his own ears.

He had fallen in love.

The most overwhelming feeling of his life—passion which defied description. And—perhaps because he had always been cynical about its existence—it hit him harder than most. He was too much in its thrall—and hers—to even try to fight it.

One night he buried his face in her scented hair as she clung to him, both of them aching and frustrated as they broke off from kissing.

He knew that she wanted him just as much as he wanted her—and he knew what he had to tell her before that happened.

'I love you, Victoria, *agape mou*.'

Her heart gave a wild leap of joy, but she looked up at him crossly. 'You don't have to tell me that just because you want to go to bed with me! I'm going to sleep with you anyway.'

'Are you?' he murmured.

'You know I am.'

He dipped his head and his lips tingled as he brushed them provocatively against hers. 'Then perhaps I will make you wait.'

'Wait?' Flagrantly, she pressed her body against his, freed by his declaration to start to explore her sexuality properly. 'Wait for what?'

'Until I make you my wife,' he said a little unsteadily—not sounding like himself at all—and Victoria stared at him with hope and disbelief. Afterwards she would realise that he hadn't actually asked her to marry him, and that he had used the word *wife* possessively—but at that moment she was too shocked and thrilled and in love to care.

'Your *wife*?'

He felt compelled by some primitive desire to tell her—some need which ran bone-deep. He had discovered the powerful lure of love and romance and its novelty made him want to plunder it to its very depths. 'Yes. We must,' he said simply. 'For it is rare for two people to feel this way—of that I am certain.'

His parents tried to stop the marriage—they summoned him home—but he resolutely ignored their demands. Even Victoria's own mother was against the union. Her proud trip to Cornwall to show him off had ended with a tearful tussle between mother and daughter after Alexei had been dispatched to buy a bottle of champagne.

'But I love him, Mum!'

'I know you do, darling,' said her mother. 'And I believe he loves you, too—but it's such early days. Marriage is difficult enough, without taking into account the fact that you're both too young and too different.'

'Is it because Dad left *you*?' questioned Victoria, and maybe that was a contributory factor to her haste. With no male figure around during her growing up years, Victoria had always seen men as distant, rather glamourous figures. The only ones she was familiar with were imaginary characters gathered from the pages of her books—and Alexei could more than match those handsome heroes.

'I just wish you would wait,' said her mother.

But they didn't want to wait, and so they married in secret—not caring who they were hurting, though in the end it was themselves they hurt the most.

Alexei took his young bride home to Athens, and that was when the fun really started.

Victoria tried to be generous—she told herself that the Christou family weren't *deliberately* trying to make her feel unwelcome—but that was how it felt.

Alexei hadn't been intending to get married, and so naturally no provision had been made for where they were going to live. Her cramped bedsit seemed like luxury in terms of privacy when compared with the prospect of moving in with his mother, his father, his two younger sisters and a whole army of silent, disapproving servants. She could imagine the way they would all look at her—this pale blonde girl who could barely speak a word of Greek.

'Can't we live on our...own?' she asked Alexei carefully.

Pride wouldn't allow him to tell her that his father was refusing to release any of his inheritance until he had proved to them that he could work for it.

'They haven't seen me properly in almost four years,' he told her instead, between kisses. 'It will be wise for us to stay with them for a time. You will feel protected here while you get to know your new country.'

Her new country—it sounded very daunting when
he put it like that, and some of the enormity of what
they had done began to slowly sink in as Victoria
was summoned before them.

'Meet my family,' said Alexei, gently propelling
her into the vast sitting room of the family villa, and
where she was greeted by several sets of lookalike
black eyes. 'This is my mother, my father—and my
two sisters.'

'K...*Kalimera,*' stumbled Victoria.

'*Kalispera!*' corrected his younger sister with a
giggle.

His mother was absolutely terrifying, and Victoria
almost felt like curtseying to her.

'How delightful to meet you, Victoria,' she said,
in cool, faintly accented English, and then deliberately spoke to her son in Greek.

Alexei frowned, and replied in the same language.

Very helpfully, his mother replied in English.
'You think so?'

A swift and heated interchange followed, and it
was only later, in the privacy of their room, that
Victoria had a chance to ask him if his mother was
angry.

Should he tell her the truth? That his mother had
accused him of throwing away his youth and op-
portunities on a hasty and ill-advised marriage to a
woman he barely knew—who couldn't speak a word
of his native tongue?

He looked down into Victoria's troubled blue eyes and tightened his arms around her. What point was there in planting discord? The two most important women in his life would soon learn to love one another.

'Come here,' he murmured. 'And let me love you.'

And when she was in his arms nothing else seemed important.

But the honeymoon couldn't last for ever. Alexei had to go to work with his father in the colossal Christou building from which their mighty shipping empire was controlled. In his efforts to prove himself, he put in long, long hours—it gave him a macho kind of buzz to always be the first one in and the last one to leave.

Victoria tried to fit in. She found herself a Greek tutor in the city, and set about making herself acceptable to Alexei's mother.

But it wasn't easy.

The only thing she did really well was cook, and the Christous already had a cook.

Her days seemed to drag, with no real role and too many empty hours to fill. With Alexei working so hard it was difficult to make new Greek friends, and she instinctively knew that if she joined an expat English enclave it would be looked down on by her in-laws.

Then Alexei came home late one night to tell her

that he was flying to New York, and she clasped her hands together with glee. At last they would be able to spend a little time alone together.

'Oooh, goody! I've never been to America before!'

Alexei's face grew shadowed. 'I am accompanying my father, Victoria *mou*. We will be conducting family business.'

Something in the way he phrased it made her realise what the answer to her question would be. 'There isn't room for your wife?'

'It is a trip for men,' he said curtly. Surely she could understand that this was a kind of apprenticeship? And then, seeing her face, he relented. 'I should bond a little with my father, *agape mou*, don't you think? He grows frail.'

She wanted to say, *I'm not surprised—he never stops working.* But she also wanted to be understanding, to be a good wife—and if he was hell-bent on a trip to the States with his father then shouldn't she let him go with a good grace?

Afterwards, she wondered if the trip had been arranged with the express purpose of parting them.

It was difficult to pinpoint exactly when Victoria realised that their marriage wasn't going anywhere. Maybe it was when the New York trip was extended. Or when his mother and sisters would stop chattering in Greek and switch to a reluctant English whenever she entered the room.

In the echoing luxury of the Christou villa there was nothing for her to do except be a wife—but her husband was missing. She felt lost, alone and adrift—and unsure what to do next.

When Alexei returned it was difficult. Formal. As if they had to start getting to know one another all over again—only they hadn't really known each other that well in the beginning. He seemed to have become remote from her—a different person from the loving partner of their carefree days in London. And his remoteness drove her even further away—made her feel she was a light-years away from him.

Victoria wasn't really surprised when Alexei told her that he and his father were going to the Far East. She wasn't even unhappy about it. It was a bit like accepting some inevitable fate—like pigging out on holiday for a fortnight and knowing that the scales were going to be way too high when you got home.

But she knew she would go mad if she played the waiting game for ever. Maybe taking a trip of her own would help her to see things clearly—to find a way forward. Or some way of going back to the way it had been.

'I'd like to go home for a while,' she told Alexei's mother one morning.

'But *this* is your home!' exclaimed Kyria Christou, and then frowned. 'And Alexei? He approves of this?'

'Oh, yes! Absolutely.' But that was an exaggeration. Alexei had sounded terse when she had told him—yet how could he possibly lecture *her* when he was thousands of miles away himself?

Victoria went to stay with her mother—whose greeting was hardly conventional. 'What's wrong?'

'Nothing's wrong! Why should it be?'

'No newlywed leaves her husband within the first year of marriage unless something's wrong.'

'I haven't *left* him,' said Victoria patiently. 'And anyway—he isn't there. He's abroad himself.' *He always is, these days.*

But it was difficult to defend a relationship which you knew deep down was balanced on precariously rocky foundations. So Victoria went to stay with Caroline, who by now was coping in a tiny flat with an overactive toddler.

'You don't know you're born!' she exclaimed, after another attempt by Victoria to convince her that being the wife of a billionaire heir wasn't all it was cracked up to be. 'Careful! You're just about to sit on some mashed apple!'

'There isn't room for me here,' Victoria said, mopping it up with a piece of kitchen roll and looking around at the toddler's clothes which were hanging on the radiators, making the atmosphere of the flat a bit like a sauna. She scooped Thomas up and sighed. 'But I don't really want to go back to Mum's—she'll just nag me.'

'Why don't you go home?'

Where was home? 'Because Alexei isn't there and his mother hates me. I'm just not good enough for her precious son.'

'What woman is?' questioned Caroline wryly. 'Why don't you go and stay with my cousin? He's got bags of room.'

Jonathan Collett did indeed have bags of room in his luxury apartment overlooking the lapping waters of London's Docklands. He was a City high-flyer, and only too pleased to have a temporary flat-mate—'Provided you do the cooking, of course!'

'Of course!'

He was charming—and good company—and Victoria knew that most women found him devastatingly attractive. But she was not most women. She was in love with another man, and furthermore she was married to him. And maybe this wasn't the way a wife should be behaving, no matter how unhappy or isolated she had grown to feel.

Soon Victoria realised it was over a week since she'd last spoken to her husband. And deep down she knew they couldn't go on like this.

She tried to contact him but when she rang the Christou house there was no reply. Should she leave a message? Victoria scraped her hand back through her hair. And say what, exactly?

Her thoughts were troubled, and she knew that she had to start taking control of her life. If there were problems then they *both* needed to address them—but they certainly couldn't carry on ignoring them.

She poured her energy into making a wonderful meal, and when Jonathan came home his face lit up in a huge smile as he undid the collar of his starchy striped shirt.

'Wow!' He sniffed appreciatively. 'What have I done to deserve this?'

'Been a fantastic landlord,' said Victoria, handing him a glass of champagne.

'Sounds like a farewell,' he commented.

'That's because it is,' said Victoria, and she couldn't miss the flash of disappointment in Jonathan's eyes. That was another problem which would be solved by her leaving. Things were getting just too comfortable here—in the easy way they often did when you weren't madly in love with a man. Simple friendship made a woman able to totally relax with a man—but the downside of that was that she then became more attractive to that man.

Oh, why was life so complicated?

The casserole was delicious, and they drank the best part of a bottle of wine, but when Jonathan put some old-fashioned Frank Sinatra on Victoria yawned, and knew that she would be asleep if she wasn't careful.

She took a shower, and afterwards was just about to make coffee, wrapped in a silky kimono with her long hair drying down her back, when the doorbell rang.

Jonathan frowned. 'Who the hell is that?'

'My X-ray vision isn't working properly tonight,' teased Victoria, scrambling to her feet. 'Don't worry—I'll get it.'

But when she opened the door she froze as if she'd seen a ghost—which in a way she had. How long had it been since her husband had stood in front of her like this? All hard-packed muscular body and eyes of jet which were...

Cold and filled with condemnation.

'Alexei,' she breathed.

'Who is it, hon?' called Jonathon.

The cold gaze flicked contemptuously over her shoulder to where Jonathan lay sprawled on the floor.

Victoria followed the direction of his eyes and saw how it must look to Alexei. The champagne. Jonathan's loosened shirt. Her lazy, contented look and the silk robe.

Her damp hair fell over her breasts as she turned back to face him. 'I know what it must look like—' she said desperately.

'You little *bitch*,' he grated.

Now was not the time to make introductions between the two men. 'We can't talk here,' she whispered, pointing towards the corridor. 'Come into my bedroom.'

But *bedroom* was obviously a bad choice of word, for his face darkened like the night as he stormed across the sitting room after her.

Alexei slammed the door shut behind them and realised that his hands were actually trembling.

'How could you?' he accused harshly.

'Alexei, I can explain—'

'How you had sex with another man?' he demanded, his voice sounding choked as he stared at the smooth surface of the duvet on the large bed and imagined the beautiful naked body of his wife grappling with another man on it.

'Of course I didn't have *sex* with him!' she protested.

His mouth twisted, along with the knife which someone had just plunged into his heart. 'What? Everything but?' he questioned with icy cruelty. 'Did he make you come with his tongue, like I do?'

'Just keep your voice down!' she said furiously, but they were interrupted by a loud knocking on the door.

'Victoria!' called Jonathan. 'Are you okay?'

Hearing the male voice was like lighting the touchpaper to Alexei's rage, and he wrenched the door open, his gaze raking contemptuously over the man who looked his very antithesis…although maybe that was what she had wanted all along. A polite, pale Englishman.

'And what are you going to do about it if she isn't?' he questioned dangerously.

Please don't say anything, Jonathan, prayed Victoria silently. But she could see him squaring up to her husband with all the effectiveness of a mouse challenging a rampaging lion.

'I'll protect her!' he vowed.

'How commendable,' bit out Alexei disdainfully. 'But I will spare your pride, my friend—since I could grind you beneath the heel of my shoe should I so desire it!' His words dripped venom and contempt in equal measure. 'Have her,' he offered silkily. 'Every cheap and cheating part of her is now yours!'

And that was when the black ice of his gaze cut through her and he said the words which had remained with her until this day—their disgust recalled in an instant. Like now.

'You are nothing but a cheap, common tramp, and I rue the day I ever married you!'

Now, seven years on, the expression on his face was pretty much as she remembered it.

Alexei's mouth curved into a bow of pure scorn. 'If it isn't the once irresistible little English sex bomb,' he murmured sarcastically. 'Why, Victoria— whatever has happened to you? You look *terrible*!'

CHAPTER FOUR

ALEXEI'S damning assessment scarcely registered, because just the impact of being in the same room as him was making Victoria feel as if someone had punched her in the stomach—hard.

That night at Jonathan's flat he had slammed out of her life—refusing to listen to her explanations then or afterwards. Her increasingly frantic letters had been sent back unopened, and he had stone-walled her attempts to speak to him. Pride had urged her not to beg his forgiveness when she knew she hadn't actually done anything wrong, yet when she tried to see what had happened through Alexei's eyes—then, yes, of course her macho, arrogant husband would have been made jealous by the scene which had confronted him that night. But she loved Alexei and only Alexei—heart, body and soul—and she needed to tell him that.

Easier said than done. Her phone calls had been taken with icy indifference by various members of the vast Christou staff, and Alexei had never returned them. She had been very effectively excluded from his life—like the outsider she had been made to feel almost from the word go. She didn't know whether or not he had been given the messages—but even if he hadn't there had been nothing to stop *him* from contacting *her*. Not if he'd really wanted to.

With a growing feeling of dismay and disbelief Victoria had finally got the message. The marriage was over. It should never really have begun.

Yet that had been seven long years ago—she should have recovered by now. So how come she was being catapulted straight back into that turmoil of emotions—anger and longing and sadness? Had all her hard work and the effort of trying to forget him all been for nothing? For why else was she fighting to stop herself from trembling beneath his cruel and candid gaze?

'Yes, terrible,' he repeated, his ebony gaze sweeping over her in brutal assessment. 'But perhaps you have a little more trouble attracting rich men these days, *ne*, Victoria?'

'What the hell are you talking about?' she whispered, shaking her head as if that could bring back some clarity of thought—something other than the trembling awareness of his muscular body.

Alexei gave a cruel smile—suddenly immensely satisfied that he had brought her here. That he could see her standing in front of him like this—her whole demeanour reinforcing what she should have known at the time.

That she was thoroughly unsuitable as a *Christou* wife!

The black eyes glittered with censure. 'Do you take no pride in your appearance any more?'

It was like a slap in the face. Victoria's eyes suddenly focussed on a large mirror which was reflecting back the Athens skyline—and the view was less forgiving than in the softly lit mirror of the lift.

Her cheap cotton sundress had looked fine when she'd put it on in England at five that morning—but the journey to the airport and the delays to the plane had left it looking like a crumpled old dishcloth. And the impossibly early hour at which she'd had to get up meant there had been no time for make-up—no time for anything, really, other than a swift face-wash and putting her long hair into a pony tail.

But she drew her shoulders back and met his stare with a defiant look of her own. Start as you mean to go on, she urged herself. Alexei is a powerful man who is used to calling the shots, and if you fall at the first hurdle you will get precisely nowhere. 'Impressing *you* wasn't top of my agenda!'

He gave a short laugh. 'You can say that again,' he agreed insultingly.

Victoria stared at him, wishing that she could say the same about him, but in all honesty she couldn't. Not that she thought for a moment that he had got out of bed that morning and thought about impressing *her*—but then, he didn't have to try. He never had.

Seven years on, Alexei had more than fulfilled the promise of his early twenties. Back then he had turned heads with his proud and arrogant beauty, but there had been a hint of the boy left behind.

Today, any trace of softness was nothing but a distant memory. He was undeniably all man—but at a cost. True, the muscular body was as hard as ever, and his lips had lost none of their sensual curve— but today they were hardened by a cynical line which made them appear cruel, and his eyes looked like pure black ice. Once he had been approach- able—today he looked utterly formidable.

She had been on her feet since before dawn, and she was tired and sticky and hungry. It was going to take a lot of effort, but she was *not* going to let him intimidate her!

'We could have sorted this out by letter!' she said furiously. '*You're* the one who forced me to come out here—so don't start complaining about it now!'

'And yet you agreed to it,' he mused, his silky voice underpinned with an iron-hard challenge. 'Why was that, I wonder—if you found the idea so abhorrent?'

'What choice did I have, Alexei?' she demanded. 'Since you seemed to find it far too adult to agree to give me a quick divorce with the minimum of fuss. I don't want a fuss—and *that's* why I'm here!'

'Ah! So time is what motivates you, is that it?' he questioned. 'A *quickie* divorce—that is what you are after, Victoria? I wonder why.' He traced the pad of his thumb thoughtfully over the sensual cushion of his lower lip.

Was he doing that on purpose? wondered Victoria. Had he discovered over the years that a woman would be mesmerised if attention was drawn to the sheer perfection of his lips? Did he realise that if that woman had also been his lover, then she'd be unable to concentrate on anything other than how it felt to have those lips roving with luxurious intimacy over the hidden places of her body? Just *stop* it, she told herself angrily. Concentrate on why you're here—not on him.

'Is there another man waiting in the wings?' he continued, his black eyes narrowing with contempt. 'Some poor sucker who you're planning to entice into wedlock? Perhaps I should warn him what he's about to take on. A fickle cheat. Still, at least I had you when you were worth having!' His smile hardened as he flicked her another glance. 'Are you carrying another man's child in your belly?'

The cruel taunt coming on top of her fatigue and turbulent emotions was the final straw, and inside Victoria snapped. All the fervent vows she'd made to herself to remain cool and not react to him just flew out of the window, and she ran at him, her hands clenched into tiny fists. 'No, I'm not!' she flared. 'And I am not a cheat!

'Want to fight me?' he murmured, holding up his own fists in a gesture of mockery. But he could not deny the relief which washed over him that another man's child was *not* growing beneath her breast. 'Come and fight me, then, *agape*.'

'I'd like to wipe that arrogant smile off your face!'

She lashed out blindly, but too late Victoria realised that she had strayed dangerously close to him. And that his proximity was acting like a stun-gun on her ability to react.

Giving a soft laugh of triumph, Alexei imprisoned her slender wrists within his hands, and—with scarcely any effort at all—he levered her up against him, her soft warmth melting against the hard, tensile length of his aroused body. Her upturned face was pale now, and her lips had begun to tremble.

'Why, Victoria,' he murmured, but he frowned— taken aback by how it felt to have her in his arms again. As if she had been made just to be held by him. He saw the magnificent blue eyes widen so that they looked as wide and as deep as the Aegean itself, and he felt his groin tighten. And if he'd been wondering if he still wanted her the answer was Yes, and yes, and a million times yes!

'Let—me—go!'

He wondered if she knew that her body was contradicting her words. That her nipples were pushing against the thin fabric of her sundress as clearly as if an artist had drawn them with a pen. He wondered if she was damp for him. Should he put his hand between her legs and discover for himself?

'But you don't want me to let go,' he whispered with silken emphasis.

She opened her mouth to speak, but no words came, and she tried to lift her hands to push him away, but they were as heavy and as lifeless as if they were made of lead.

How could the simple contact of two bodies be so devastating? As if it had started some blazing fire within her blood? Victoria felt her face begin to heat, felt herself begin to sink against him. She could not seem to prevent herself—as if her actions were beyond any kind of conscious control. Her body was reacting to him as it always had done in the past—call it habit or call it instinct; it simply hadn't had time to reprogramme itself, that was all. The prickling of her breasts and her skin and the heavy pulsing of her blood happened as automatically as breathing whenever she was around him.

Alexei found himself growing even harder—so hard that he felt he might explode with it. He had intended to demonstrate his superior resolve by holding her close like this—to show both of them that he was able to resist her. And yet...and yet...

'Oh, God,' he grated helplessly, and he found

himself weakening. With an angry groan he drove his lips down on hers in a punishing kiss.

It should have repelled her—and in one way it did, for the kiss bore no resemblance to its tender cousin of their courting days. This kiss was hard and deliberately provocative—a demonstration of power, not affection. It was designed to excite feeling, not to express emotion. It was the kiss of a seasoned master—applied with just the right amount of pressure and just the right level of a sigh so that when Victoria's lips opened beneath his, he gave a little moan of triumph.

She allowed herself a brief moment of intimacy as their tongues mingled like old friends who had been parted for too long. It was pure enchantment of the senses, and Victoria wrapped her arms around his neck almost without having realised she had done it. But surely on one level she could be understood—if not forgiven? He was so deliciously familiar—everything about him—his smell and the feel of his body and the taste of his mouth.

And you want him—you want him still... Even after all this time it takes just one touch to have you drowning in pleasure. You want him to drive his strong, virile body into yours—his hard, sure rhythm taking you to that place where everything is obliterated except sensation itself.

For a moment she allowed herself the wild fantasy of imagining him peeling down her panties—or, even more likely, impatiently pushing the flimsy fabric aside. And lying her on the desk to straddle her, before unzipping himself to thrust long and hard and deep within her.

But the image appalled her even while it excited her, and she opened her eyes to find that his were glittering at her—black and calculating, like a master chess player plotting his next move. And the fact that he hadn't even been moved enough to close his eyes was enough to break the enchantment.

Somehow Victoria found the strength to tear herself away, and she stood staring at him with anger, her breathing laboured and her throat dry—frustrated desire making dark pools of her blue eyes.

'Stopping before the fun really starts?' he queried.

Frantically she smoothed her hands over her flaming cheeks. 'What the hell was that all about?' she demanded hoarsely.

'Do you really have to ask?' He arched his eyebrows arrogantly. 'Doesn't it strike you as frustrating that desire can be the last thing to die—even when respect and affection have fled?'

On legs which felt as if they were made of jelly Victoria walked over to the opposite side of the office, aware that she was trembling from head to toe, that her cheeks were flushed and that she was furious with herself. Oh, why hadn't she *stopped* him? Or kept her mouth shut? Or pushed him away? Or slapped his face? Instead of melting and virtually opening her legs for him, begging that he do it to her there and then?

'I can't believe you just did that,' she said in a small voice.

His eyes raked over her with predatory appreciation. 'Then your knowledge of men is remarkably lacking,' he said softly.

'And I can't believe I just let you.'

'Then your knowledge of yourself must be equally deficient, Victoria *mou*, when we both know how delightfully easy it is to turn you on.'

'You don't even *like* me,' she stated flatly. She turned to face him again, braving whatever she would read in his eyes—though wasn't there a part of her which secretly hoped he'd deny it? Say that he'd never stopped loving her and never would? And even if he couldn't bring himself to say that then maybe he'd come out with one of those phrases people always used in television dramas—about how deep down he would always like and respect her simply because she had been his wife.

But he didn't, of course.

'Men don't have to like a woman to want to have sex with them. Surely you know *that*, Victoria? They just have to be with a woman who will...'

He finished the sentence in Greek, but Victoria didn't need to be a linguist to know that it was earthy, and crude. And harsh.

'How delightfully you put it!' she observed sarcastically, but his words hurt—as he had intended them to. If wounding was his game then he was winning, because the contrast between talking about 'wanting sex' and their blissful lovemaking of the past was almost too poignant to bear.

'I'm not a diplomat,' he mused, as the aching began to subside by a fraction. 'After all, you are still my wife, and as long as you remain so I have certain rights.'

'*Rights?*' Victoria stared at him. 'What kind of rights?'

He leaned back against his desk, his long legs stretched out in front of him. 'Oh, please don't play the naïve little virgin with me, Victoria! Not when we know how many times you've been around the block and back again!'

'That's not true!' she protested, stung.

'And the man I found you with? Half-naked and alone? Was he a figment of my imagination?' Even now just the mention of that night was like a knife ripping through his guts and leaving his entrails to be picked over by vultures.

'It wasn't like that! I didn't do anything wrong. I was married to you at the time—I was your *wife*!' She could hear her voice sounding almost pleading, but the look in Alexei's cold eyes was merciless.

'You expect me to believe that?' he drawled arrogantly. 'You, who are always so hot and hungry for sex? You couldn't wait to leap into bed with *me*,

could you? So why should I flatter myself into thinking it would be different for anyone else?' Alexei
realised the scar of her betrayal was as deep and as
raw in him as ever it had been. Why else would he
still feel this same hot, overpowering rage after so
many years and so many women? Did that explain
this desire to have her submit to him? To punish her
in some way—to wound her with his tongue the way
she had wounded him with her body?

His face was unsmiling as he stared at her mouth
very deliberately. 'But you are right about one
thing—you *were* my wife, and in name you still
are. And we both know exactly what kind of rights
I'm talking about. Shall we do it now—here?'
Suggestively he let his tongue snake provocatively
around his lips. 'Even if it's for the very last time?'

'You're…you're *barbaric*!' she accused unsteadily, though her eyes were mesmerised by the
movement of his lips—like a rabbit made helpless
by the blinding headlights of an oncoming car. 'A
savage! Men don't come out with statements like
that in the civilised world!'

'Or maybe I'm just honest?' he parried. 'I know
it's not one of your strong points, but I'm a big fan
of honesty. And who cares about being civilised,
agape mou? My being a real man always turned you
on—and it still does. You want me now as much as
I do you. You're wet for me, Victoria, you know
you are.'

'Shut up!' she moaned.

He watched as she raked her hand through her fringe in a gesture he recognised of old. She was angry, yes—but he was right. She was frustrated, too. Hovering on the knife-edge of desire. One touch, and...

He studied her dispassionately. Her hair was no longer the white-blonde colour it had become when bleached from living beneath the fierce Grecian sun, but it still fell like a pale waterfall almost to her waist. How he had loved to encircle that tiny waist and then rub his thumb down over her belly, down between her legs. He remembered how she would squirm, how he had perfected the art of bringing her to orgasm discreetly. How he had taught her everything he knew about sex.

Sometimes it had thrilled them to be sitting in some semi-public place while his hand slipped underneath the skirt or dress he'd always insisted she wore, and Victoria would bite down hard on his shoulder as she convulsed ecstatically beneath his fingers.

Her cheeks flamed. 'Stop looking at me that way!'

'What way is that, Victoria?'

'You know what way!' she said, trying to stop her voice from shaking—though from desire or indignation she wasn't quite sure. 'It's predatory. It's insulting—and I don't like it!'

'Liar,' he whispered.

Victoria knew that she had to pull herself together—to step back from the sensual snare he had set before it was too late. 'I'm not having this discussion,' she said quietly. 'I came here to talk about my divorce—as requested by *you*. It was a journey I could have happily done without and I'd like to tie it up as quickly as possible.' She looked at him. 'So, shall we get on with it?'

'Not now, I'm afraid.' He glanced at his watch—a platinum extravagance which gleamed quietly against his olive skin. 'I have a meeting scheduled.'

Was this another kind of power game? Victoria narrowed her eyes. Alexei had known she was coming here today—but of course she couldn't *force* him to talk to her, so, yes, of *course* it was a power game. She was on his territory—a place where he could call all the shots. Well, she would be dignified. She would speak to him courteously—even though he *was* a barbaric savage.

'Okay,' she said steadily. 'What time can you see me?'

'Why don't I pick you up for dinner?'

'Dinner wasn't what I had in mind.'

'Tough. You have to eat, and so do I.'

'Since you put it so nicely.' Victoria bared her teeth in a sarcastic imitation of a smile, because she knew from that ruthless look on his face that she was beaten. 'Dinner would be *wonderful*.'

Sarcasm was something that didn't feature in

Alexei's life, and a nerve at his cheek briefly flickered in irritation. Didn't she have any idea of how many women would move mountains to get a dinner invitation from him? His irritation banished, he feasted his eyes on the way the cheap little dress clung to the high curve of her buttocks and wondered if she still wore those tiny lacy panties. 'Where are you staying?' he drawled.

What *was* the name of the place? Feeling all fingers and thumbs under his blatantly sexual scrutiny, she pulled a computer print-out from her handbag and pointed to the name of her hotel. 'Here…I'm not sure how to pronounce it.'

Alexei's took the paper from her, his black brows knitting together as he scanned it. 'Who booked this?' he demanded.

'I did, of course—*I* haven't got a troop of staff to do it for me! On the internet.'

'On the *internet*?' he repeated incredulously, as if he couldn't quite believe that this was what people did.

But then, he didn't live like normal people did, Victoria reminded herself. That was one of Alexei's problems—he didn't apply the rules of normal people to himself, either. Maybe he didn't feel he needed to. With power and prestige like his, it must be like finding yourself on some lofty Olympian mountain. Surrounded by beauty, but ultimately alone. 'Yes, Alexei. On the internet.'

'Well, you are not staying there,' he snapped.

'Oh, but I am!'

'No, you are *not*, Victoria!' His eyes grew flinty. 'Do you know anything about this area?'

'In my parallel life as a Greek tourist guide, you mean?' she questioned sardonically, pleased to see the fury in his eyes intensify. 'It's not one I'm familiar with, no. What's wrong with it?'

'What's wrong with it? Everything! It's dangerous and it's rough. And, furthermore, it's on the very far side of the city—an area I never visit and do not intend to! I will *not* have my wife staying there!'

'Shouldn't that be up to me?' she snapped. 'I can do exactly as I please and stay exactly *where* I please!'

'Normally, yes,' he agreed tightly. 'In any other country or city in the world—but not in *my* city. Can you just imagine what the newspapers would say if they discovered that a Christou was staying in a...a *hovel*?'

'So that's what this is all about, is it?' she raged. 'Your image?'

'No, Victoria, it is *not* about image—it is about the pride of the family name! Which, until the divorce papers are signed, remains *your* name, too!'

She had forgotten how *autocratic* he could be. At nineteen, and completely besotted, she had been prepared to go along with it—but seven years on Victoria found it intolerable. 'You can't stop me!'

He paused, and when he spoke his voice was deadly soft. 'No, you're right. I can't—but I can prove very difficult if you choose to defy me, Victoria. Either you stay somewhere which meets with my approval and which conforms to your position as my wife, or you can kiss your swift settlement goodbye.' He shrugged. 'The choice is yours.'

She stared at him. 'What kind of choice is that?' she whispered. 'That's blackmail!'

'I would prefer to call it tough negotiation,' he parried smoothly. 'Or concern for your welfare.'

Like hell it was—he would probably have thrown her to the wolves if he could! Victoria stared at him, feeling completely and utterly trapped. But then, that was nothing new. When he'd left her alone as a young bride, in a strange country surrounded by his unfriendly family, hadn't she felt exactly the same? The circumstances might have changed, but the feeling hadn't—this dominant man was taking control and pulling the strings of her life. And, just like back then, she was powerless against him—as usual, Alexei was calling all the shots.

'Haven't you forgotten something? I can't afford five-star hotels,' she said quietly.

Now, this was the kind of negotiation he *could* deal with! She was in no position to fight him on this—he knew it, and she knew it, too. 'No, but I can. It will be my gift to you, and you will accept it.'

Even in spite of her plight she was unable to resist. 'But I was always taught to beware of Greeks bearing gifts!'

His smile was instinctive, but afterwards he felt angry—as if it had shown a weakness in him. He would *not* let the witch use humour to soften him! 'I will have my assistant book you into the Astronome and pick you up at eight.' He cast a disparaging look over her woefully small bag. 'Oh, and you'd better give Room Service a call and get them to press your *finery*,' he suggested with silky sarcasm. 'I'm sure you've brought lots of it with you.'

CHAPTER FIVE

VICTORIA was still seething as she unpacked her bag in a suite which was as big as an aircraft hanger. She couldn't bear to think how much a place like this was costing. It didn't matter that Alexei could afford to buy the hotel if he wanted to—it still made her beholden to him when she didn't want to be. And the image of his mocking face was stubbornly refusing to shift.

How dared he rubbish everything she was and everything she stood for? Looking down his arrogant nose at her as if she were a piece of something unmentionable he'd picked up off his shoe just because she didn't want to spend a year's salary on a hotel room? At least she'd worked all her life, and everything she had—she'd earned the hard way. She hadn't been handed lavish riches by virtue of an accident of birth.

But it was pointless getting angry. Alexei wasn't even here, and—let's face it—she had allowed him to move her here without kicking up too much of a fight. Was that because luxury like this was powerfully seductive? Glancing around her, Victoria allowed herself a moment to revel in the kind of place which was second nature to the Christou family. *Of course it was.*

The Astronome had such a picture-perfect view of the famous Acropolis that it felt as if she was looking out onto a postcard. Lavish and scented displays of flowers were dotted around the suite, along with bowls of wonderful fruit. There were irresistible dark chocolates and bottles of vintage champagne stacked in the fridge—and just when Victoria thought it couldn't possibly get any more luxurious she noticed a flat-screen TV as big as a cinema screen and a Jacuzzi outside on the wide terrace, overlooking the city.

And there, lying in stark and shabby contrast on the bed where she'd unpacked it, was her entire holiday wardrobe. There wasn't very much…a denim mini-skirt, three-for-the-price-of-two T-shirts, three chainstore dresses, a bikini and a cardigan. Very cheap and not terribly cheerful—and didn't it just show?

Victoria rang the laundry service to have them whisked away, and by the time she'd finished showering there was a rap on the door and her clothes were returned—looking about a million times better than when they'd left.

Which wasn't saying much.

Still, she was not aiming to be something she wasn't. She was a hard-working and self-supporting young woman and proud of it. So sock it to him, Victoria.

Her hair she left loose, save for two small blue clips which pinned the heavy swathes away from her face and matched her cotton sundress. Her hooped earrings might be plastic, but they were the exact colour of the dress, as were the bangles which clinked at her narrow wrist.

Victoria did a twirl in front of the mirror. Not bad. Not bad at all. Was the dress too short? Were too much of her legs on show?

Who cared?

Defiantly, she applied another coat of mascara—half knowing but not caring what Alexei would think of her appearance. It was nothing to do with him *what* she wore. Ultra-short was the current skirt length—especially in a climate like this one—and she certainly was *not* trying to please her old-fashioned, soon-to-be-ex-husband!

But her bravado slipped a little as she made her way to the hotel's rooftop restaurant where she was meeting him. She knew that she stuck out like a sore thumb among the expensive designer clothes of the other women. Pure silks and satins gleamed expensively in the discreet candlelight, and bony fingers were weighted down with diamonds like small chunks of ice.

She felt like a child who had wandered into a grown-ups' party by mistake and, now she was here, didn't quite know what game everyone else was playing.

Well, you hold your head up high, for a start. You remember that once you, too, were a part of this world—but you chose to reject it. Or rather, it rejected you. It's only money, and money means nothing. The things that counted were real feelings and genuine emotions—and they had been in short enough supply with Alexei once the first flush of lust had dissolved.

She turned her head, as if knowing exactly where he would be sitting. And, yes—there he was. It was almost as if she had some sixth sense where he was concerned, and that in itself spooked her. And how annoying, but how predictable, that her heart should miss a beat as she looked at him—alone at what was clearly the best table, with the fading light of a magnificent sunset lighting the sky behind him.

Behind the thin skin at her temple she could feel the now rapid hammering of her pulse and was aware that her breathing had grown shallow—all physical manifestations of desire, which she couldn't do a thing about. Except try to disguise it. Because how could she have forgotten what the sight of Alexei in a dinner suit did to her equilibrium?

And not just hers, judging by the fan-club of women who were trying not to stare at him in the way that sophisticated people did when they were pretending not to have noticed someone spectacular in their midst.

Black suited him. The stark colour accentuated the broad shoulders and the muscular thrust of his limbs.

Aware of the envious glances which were being cast her way, Victoria followed the head waiter to Alexei's table and came to a halt in front of him, wishing that she could shake off the feeling of being some kind of concubine who had been produced to satisfy the desire of her master.

'Hello, Alexei,' she said coolly, marvelling at how she could manage to disguise her voice so that it gave away nothing of the impact he was having on her. 'Have you been waiting long?'

He rose while the waiters fussed around her until she was seated, and then sank down opposite. 'Exactly twenty minutes—because that's how late you are,' he murmured silkily. 'Did it give you pleasure to leave me cooling my heels?'

'I didn't give it a thought.' And that was no lie. She'd been so busy trying to look as good as possible that she hadn't realised that time had flown.

He had been aware of how it must look to the other diners—Alexei Christou, sitting alone at a table for so long that he might almost have been stood up. The idea of *that* was preposterous! And yet, wasn't there a bit of him which wouldn't have been surprised if she *had* decided not to show? If she'd called his bluff and left an angry note for him before flying straight back to London?

And hadn't that excited him? For there was an unpredictable side to Victoria's nature which fascinated as much as infuriated him.

She must want this deal really badly, he thought, if she was prepared to accept his offer of a luxury hotel suite and the demand that she have dinner with him. And if she wanted something really badly, then that put him in a position of strength.

Just how far would she be prepared to go to get it? he wondered idly, a pulse in his groin beginning to beat steadily as he drank in her appearance like a man who had spent too long in the desert.

He had watched her as she sashayed across the room towards him—observing the effect she had on every male occupant of the room, even though she seemed to be oblivious to the stir of interest she was creating. And it had not pleased him.

Her dress was too cheap and too short, and her sparkly sandals looked like those that tourists purchased from the cut-price stalls in the marketplace. Never had a woman sharing his table looked more unsuitable, and he should have found it easy not to want her. And yet…yet…

Damn it—but he could take her over the table in an instant!

What was it about sexual chemistry? About the components which made a female utterly desirable?

Compared to the other women in the restaurant she looked cheaply dressed, and yet she had something all the money in the world couldn't buy.

Her casual hair had all the dreamy promise of bed. He wanted to tangle his hands in it, wrap strands of it around his fingers, imprisoning her so that he could do with her what he wished... Alexei felt the hot thrust of desire, felt the tight rod of his erection as it nudged against him. And soon Victoria would feel it, too. He would fill her with his manhood while she begged for him never to stop.

'Perhaps you deliberately kept me waiting?' he murmured. 'Were you hoping I'd go away?'

Victoria met his smile with a glacial version of her own. 'Tempting though that is—in this case it wouldn't help. I'm afraid that this meeting is something that has to be endured,' she answered sweetly. 'Like having a tooth pulled.'

'You are already late, and I am prepared to tolerate *one* rudeness this evening—but no more than that,' he warned. But again—infuriatingly—that bubbling up of laughter was lurking dangerously in the background. And then his black eyes glinted dangerously as he saw a man look across at her as if he would like to...

Resisting the desire to go over and pick the insolent voyeur up by the collar and throw him out of the elegant room, he directed his fury towards Victoria instead. But she hadn't even noticed!

Instead, she had bent her head and was studying the menu—when he was still in the middle of having a conversation with her!

'Hungry?' he queried sarcastically.

Victoria looked up from her menu, where she had been seeking refuge from the disturbing scrutiny of his gaze. 'Starving,' she answered truthfully. The movement sent her hair shimmering down her back, so that all his attention was drawn to the points of her breasts which were showing clearly through the thin fabric. No wonder the other men were leering at her so openly!

He leaned forward, his face close enough for her to see the ebony spark of anger in his eyes. 'Just why are you dressed like that?' he demanded.

'Like what?'

Oh, those big blue eyes, and that sham look of innocence. She might have been innocent when first he had met her, but once she had tasted the joy of sex she had never looked back. He had watched the tight bud of her sexuality burst open into a blowsy and responsive flower. How quickly she had learnt to listen to and enjoy the pleasure signals of her body. And how many men had tasted her perfect sensual beauty since he had awoken it? he wondered jealously.

'You are wearing too much make-up and your skirt is indecent!' he grated.

Victoria shrugged. 'It's fashionable,' she said easily. 'And I can wear what I want.'

'You look like a tramp!' he breathed. 'A whore! Was that your intention?'

'I thought that was what you thought I was anyway—or so you once told me! And please do modify your language, Alexei. We're not alone now, and people can hear what you're saying.' Victoria smiled up at the waiter with a complicit look of resignation before leaning forward to speak softly. 'We don't want everyone to think we're conducting some kind of sexual negotiation, do we?'

Rarely had Alexei felt such pure, impotent rage as he did at that moment. He felt the faint tremble of his hand and he found himself wanting to hull her to her cheaply shod feet and to kiss her hard and strong until she melted. And then carry her out of this restaurant with everyone staring at him jealously, knowing exactly what it was he intended to do to her...

'Are you all right, Alexei?' questioned Victoria softly. 'Because beneath that lovely tan you've gone almost pale!'

His eyes narrowed in suspicion. Taunting him by sending out blatantly sexual signals or innocently enquiring after his health? Which? Was she just playing games with him?

Of course she was! In the past, he had been her willing sexual slave, and that, of course, was her most powerful weapon. He had let his guard down with her in a way he had never done before—nor since—and now bitterly regretted.

But he must not forget that she was now his adversary, and no different from any other enemy—business or personal. The only sure-fire method of always coming out on top was to ensure that you took control and never showed weakness. Not this time, he thought grimly. Not this time.

Not taking his eyes from her face, he ran a long finger around his collar. 'I was getting a little… *zestos* underneath the collar.' Deliberately he snaked his tongue along his bottom lip, as if he were running it along the inside of her thigh, and watched her blue eyes dilate in helpless response. He felt the power shift yet again. Yes! She might play her little games, but she wanted him still! He would have her in his bed before the night was out, and he would see for himself if she was as good as he remembered. He would take his fill of her, and then he would send her packing.

Noticing that her cheeks were flushed, he leaned forward. 'And now it is my turn to question whether *you* are all right, *agape mou*? For your face has grown a little heated. Perhaps it is a little too hot for both of us, *ne*? Shall we go and stand together at the far end of the terrace, where no one can see us? There the evening breeze can cool your skin like a man's breath—would you like that?'

Victoria sipped water through bone-dry lips, willing herself not to respond. What a consummate master of words he could be! Pretending concern while his eyes flashed a message of unashamed sensuality. He knew exactly what he was doing. Pushing her just to see how far she would go. Oh, yes—Alexei knew all the right buttons to press. He knew exactly how to get under her skin.

'That won't be necessary,' she said. 'I'll feel better once I've got some food inside me.'

'Wouldn't you rather have *me* inside you?'

'You're disgusting!'

'What's wrong with a simple question like that? Ever since you walked in you've been feasting your eyes upon me like a starving woman who has not been fed in a long, long time.'

She met his eyes, braved their hostile light—but she could not deny the truth behind his words. 'Your physical allure was never in dispute, Alexei.'

'Nor yours,' he said silkily. 'So, how long is it since you *have* been fed, Victoria?'

'I had a sandwich on the aeroplane,' she said deliberately.

'That wasn't what I meant and you know it.' His voice was throaty and he lowered it until it was a husky enticement. 'What about those other, more ancient hungers, *agape mou*? How long is it since a man has been between your honeyed thighs? Plunging deep and deeper still into your moist, sweet cavern? Thrusting over and over again until you sob out your pleasure beneath him? How long?' The black brows curved upwards in arrogant query.

Despite her resolve not to let him get under her skin, Victoria felt herself tremble with a combination of humiliation and hunger—because only a liar would have denied the fact that his words excited as well as insulted her. She lowered her voice. 'Do you want me to walk out of this restaurant right now?'

'But then you risk going away empty-handed. I thought we were supposed to be discussing the terms of our divorce.'

'I'm beginning to wonder if it's worth it if you're going to sit there making vile sexual innuendo all evening,' she said flatly.

'Then go. Let the lawyers deal with it.'

He was calling her bluff. Damn him! Victoria shook her head. 'I haven't come all this way just to turn around and go home. Shall we get ordering out of the way?'

Alexei spoke in rapid Greek to the waiter. 'Still like fish?' he asked her, suddenly switching to such a normal voice that for one bizarre moment it felt just like a proper dinner date.

Victoria nodded.

'Here, they do the best fish in the city.'

Of course, if this *were* any other meal with any other man, she would make a polite noise of appreciation. But it wasn't. It was something to be endured and then ended as soon as was humanly possible.

There was a brief silence as bread and olives were brought and cold white wine poured. Victoria hadn't been planning to drink alcohol, but suddenly she felt a need of something—anything—to help her through the ordeal ahead. The candlelight was playing on his black hair and casting shadows over his chiselled features, and pinpoints of light glittered in the depths of his dark eyes.

In a way it was an intimate setting, and yet it was deeply unsettling because of the hostility and the tension which were simmering beneath the surface. Suddenly she didn't really know where to begin. And—from the expectant and sarcastic look on his cruel face—he didn't intend to help her.

'I'm waiting, Victoria,' he said softly.

She put the glass down. 'I don't intend to be greedy.'

His eyes were stony. 'Let's skip the niceties, shall we? Just cut to the chase. *I'll* decide whether or not your demand is excessive.'

He looked so dark and broodingly Greek that it was sometimes easy to forget that he was a truly cosmopolitan man—but his sarcastic words reminded her that he had been educated in English and French, as well as Greek. 'My lawyer said to give you this.' She reached into her bag and produced a letter, which she placed in front of him.

He picked it up and scanned it, and his face was impassive when he looked up. As a race, Greek men learned early never to let their feelings show—especially during business transactions—and Alexei had learnt the lesson well, a dream pupil. What a little fool she was—and what an idiot her lawyer! Did they not realise that this demand was almost laughable in its modesty? That it could have been multiplied by ten and then by ten again and still not have made a dent in his colossal fortune?

He folded the letter carefully and put it into the pocket of his jacket. 'Such a sum will make a difference to you?'

Victoria nodded. It would make all the difference in the world, but he did not need to know that. 'Yes,' she answered quietly.

He ate an olive, scraping the flesh away with his teeth and placing the stripped stone in the dish in front of them. There was something almost erotic about the act, and he watched the slow rise of colour to her cheeks, his glittering black gaze never leaving her face.

'And just how badly do you want the money?' he questioned softly.

'I'm not going to beg, if that's what you're hoping for. It's a fair entitlement.'

Very fair. He almost laughed aloud. 'But perhaps

I can tempt you with more? You can have double the amount you've asked for, Victoria—perhaps I'll even triple it,' he added magnanimously. 'What would you say to that?'

Her eyes narrowed in suspicion. 'You're giving me more than I asked for—for *nothing*?' she whispered.

And then he did laugh—but it was a sound filled with cold venom instead of mirth. What a naïve little fool she was beneath her cheap, tramp-like exterior. 'Oh, no—not for nothing,' he emphasised silkily. 'Don't you know that everything in life has its price, *agape mou*? We just have to agree on what that price is.'

'I'm…I'm not with you.'

He paused before delivering his final blow. 'Become my mistress for a week and you can write your own cheque, Victoria—and walk away from Athens a very rich woman.'

CHAPTER SIX

Across the candlelit table, Victoria scarcely noticed the plates of fish the waiter was putting down in front of them. She swallowed down the sour taste in her mouth and stared at the harshly beautiful features of the man who sat opposite her.

Had she misheard him? Could the man who had once loved her enough to make her his wife have really just offered her money for sex? As if she really was some kind of...

She searched his face, as if expecting him to suddenly burst out laughing—the way he might have done once, a long time ago—to tell her that he had been having a wicked joke at her expense. But the Alexei of today did not laugh—and certainly not with her. That time was past, and his mouth was not smiling, merely quizzical, while the expression in his brilliant black eyes was coldly calculating. And it told her that he had been deadly serious.

'Are you trying to insult me?' she demanded on a shaky whisper.

'Insult you?' Alexei looked at her impatiently. 'How like a woman to pitch it at the wrong emotional level! *Ochi*, Victoria—I am simply trying to negotiate a deal.'

'By treating your wife like a…like a…*hooker*?' she whispered.

He shrugged. 'What's wrong with hookers? I'm *told* that they're easy to do business with—particularly high-class ones. They deliver the goods without any unrealistic emotional expectations. I thought that was why you'd dressed that way tonight!'

'You're a pig!'

He sat back in his chair and enjoyed the outrage. It shaped her mouth into a glistening pink bow which looked as if were just about to let forth a torrent of invective. 'Ah, come, come, *oreos mou*— there is no need for a scene. We are already causing enough interest. A simple yes or no will be sufficient.' His black eyes glittered with provocation. 'It's only sex after all, Victoria—something we have done time and time again with undeniable enjoyment. And who knows? The novelty of introducing payment for the transaction could add an extra dimension of excitement.'

'Why are you doing this?' she breathed.

'Why do you think?' Instinct told Alexei to hide his desire for revenge from her. If he told her that he wanted to extract retribution from her for having humiliated him with another man then would that not make him appear emotionally vulnerable in her eyes?

His eyes glittered as he reached for another equally valid reason. 'Because, unfortunately, I still find you desirable,' he drawled. 'And I left before I had taken my fill of you. Perhaps I want to remedy that while I have this heaven-sent opportunity. Like a man who tumbles upon an unexpected spring and finds that he is still thirsty.' His eyes became smoky, his voice a velvety caress. 'Maybe I want to know if you're as hot as you were all those years ago.'

If only he knew!

Yet, in spite of her outrage at his comments, Victoria could feel the unwelcome prickling of her breasts and the slow flush of her cheeks. Long-forgotten pleasures of the flesh began to clamour to make themselves heard. Pleasures which had simply lain dormant because no other man had come close to unlocking them.

She shook her head, like a swimmer who had emerged from the water temporarily deafened. 'You can go to hell!' she blurted out.

'Is that a no?'

'It's a never!'

'Bad choice of word, *agape mou*,' he purred. 'You may live to regret having said it.'

'The only thing I regret is having met you in the first place!'

And suddenly his features hardened so that it was like looking at the face of some dark statue—a fallen angel. Beauty made harsh by contempt.

'Then at least there's one thing we agree on,' he grated.

'I can't stay here!' she said desperately, knowing that she couldn't bear to have everything they'd ever shared rubbished over a dinner table. Pushing back her chair, she scrambled to her feet—not caring that the other diners were looking at them, startled. 'I'm not listening to another word of this!'

'Sit down,' he gritted, because—improbably—he could see that she meant it.

'And subject myself to more of this? I don't think so, Alexei! You can go to hell.'

Victoria stumbled out of the restaurant, and if she hadn't been quite so upset then she might have found the expression on the faces of the waiters and other diners almost comical. As if they were unable to believe that someone had just walked out on Kyrios Christou, leaving the handsome billionaire sitting fuming at a restaurant table.

She took the stairs instead of the lift, feeling just like Cinderella leaving the glitzy ballroom in rags. But wasn't Cinderella exactly what she was—what she always had been to Alexei? The poor girl plucked out of obscurity by the rich man and then set back down there again, according to his whim. Staying in a place which probably cost as much per night as she earned in a month cooking for executives—if she was lucky.

She pulled out her room-key, but her fingers were trembling so much that she couldn't get it in the lock—and then she heard a horribly familiar voice behind her which made her blood run cold.

'Allow me,' came the silken purr, and Victoria whirled round to stare incredulously at the unrepentant face of Alexei.

'G-get out of here!' she breathed.

But he ignored her. Plucking the key from her fingers, he unlocked the door, gently pushing her inside the suite and closing the door behind him. It was an overwhelmingly masterful action—reminding her that although he might have been educated in America inside he was all autocratic and macho Greek.

So do something.

Kick him out.

Call security.

Victoria stared at him, her breath coming thick and fast in her throat when she saw the look of intent in his dark eyes. But she must be mistaken…she must be… She had just told him unequivocally what she thought of his suggestion.

He had loosened his tie and was stretching his head and shoulders in some horrible parody of an aching husband returning home after a hard day's work. But they had never done normal stuff like that. And now he was…was…

'What do you think you're doing?' She swallowed as he began to shrug out of his jacket. She could see the faint outline of his hard torso beneath his white silk shirt.

'Oh, come on, Victoria—we were in the middle of a conversation.' His black eyes glittered. 'I think we ought to finish it, don't you?'

'So talking involves taking your clothes off, does it?' she demanded.

He raised his eyebrows in a mocking parody of a question. 'Well, it *was* just my jacket—but I can always remove more if you really want me to.'

'You're disgusting! I don't even know why you've bothered following me, because I've got nothing to say to you!'

'*Ochi?* Are you sure, Victoria *mou*?' And without warning he put his arms around her, just as he had done earlier in his office. This time she should have been prepared. She should have stopped him—but, just like earlier, she melted into him like butter on hot toast, her soft body fitting perfectly against the hard length of his as if someone had designed them for just that purpose.

'I've got nothing to say to you,' she repeated unconvincingly.

Her breath was warm on his cheek as she half-pushed, half-clung to his chest, and he knew she didn't want to go anywhere. And neither did he. 'Then maybe the time for words is past,' he murmured.

'Don't.' But she sounded like someone saying she

shouldn't have that piece of chocolate cake when it was already on its glistening way to her mouth.

He smiled. 'But you want me.'

'No. No, I don't.'

He tipped up her face and saw the rapid play of emotions which passed over her features like clouds moving swiftly across the face of the sun. Until only one remained—one which was stronger than all the others, as strong and as powerful as life itself—for without it there would be no life.

Desire.

'Yes,' he breathed. 'Oh, yes, you do. I can feel it—and I want it, too.' And then he could hold out no longer. 'Victoria,' he groaned, and he crushed his mouth down onto hers, tasting its berry-sweetness and the slick moistness of her lips.

Victoria felt like a champagne bottle which someone had been shaking before unexpectedly popping the cork. But instead of an explosion of sparkling wine it was a tumult of feelings which rushed out and spilled over, and there didn't seem to be a thing she could do about it. It was just pure sensation, one after another, an unremitting onslaught on the senses which left her reeling.

He dragged his mouth away from hers. 'Victoria!' he groaned again, and this time that half-familiar sound worked its own kind of dark magic on her senses. Some distant trigger from long ago in the way he said her name made the sharp yearning even more intense. Because his voice hadn't changed—it was still silky-deep and accented, and he still said it like nobody else—emphasising the second syllable, running his tongue around it as if it were fine wine.

'We...*mustn't*,' she breathed. But maybe by then it was already too late—for didn't the way she'd phrased it imply collusion between the two of them? *We* mustn't. As if they had planned it together. Well, maybe they had—on some deep and subconscious level. Because things could have been very different.

She could have got her lawyer to ring him.

She needn't have come out to Greece on his say-so.

But then, he hadn't had to invite her.

He could have scheduled this meeting in the imposing atmosphere of his vast office—not over dinner in an exclusive restaurant.

And even if all those things had failed she still could have told him to go away, to have meant it and sounded like she meant it. But instead she was leaning into him, close as a shaving of lead which had latched onto a great big magnet. And now he had begun to tangle his hands in her hair—like in days gone by and her head was tipping back and she was closing her eyes, praying for him not to stop.

'Oh, God!' she gasped.

Alexei gave a small cry of delight, sensing her capitulation as he began to plant butterfly kisses on her neck, feeling her body begin to tremble uncontrollably as he moved his mouth towards the shadowed hollow in her throat. He wanted to prolong this teasing foreplay that hinted at the intense pleasures to come—until it was so unbearable that they would both be begging for release—but his normally rigid sense of control seemed to have deserted him.

He put his hand up her dress and she squealed aloud, bucking like a mule as his fingertips alighted on her moist panties—their heat almost searing him. And...*ghlikos*...thank heavens he was holding onto her waist, for her knees sagged and she would have fallen otherwise.

'Victoria,' he groaned, and lay her down on the cool marble floor as carefully as if she had been made of glass—though glass was cold and she was all living and breathing fire beneath his touch.

Heatedly, she stared up at him—her head spinning as if she was in the middle of a fever. Her hands sprang to his shoulders—though she wasn't quite sure whether she should cling on or push him away. Something deep inside her—some last vestige of reason—told her that this was all wrong. That she should stop him—and stop him now. For, while Alexei was a powerful man with a vast sexual appetite, he would not take her by force—his pride would not let him.

And yet some emotion which went far deeper than reason kept her holding him. 'Alexei,' she whimpered, and she closed her eyes before he could read the pain in them.

He could see the torn expression on her face even while she parted her thighs for him, and he could barely speak—his throat felt thick and constricted. And not just his throat.

'You want me to go?' he demanded. 'You want me to stop this? To leave you like this?'

Her eyes fluttered open and he was all muscle and tension—his face tight with concentration. She could see that he was gearing up to stop, that all it would take would be one word from her.

'Do you?' he demanded. 'For God's sake tell me now, Victoria—or else I will die with the waiting and the wanting.'

And maybe his poetic choice of words drove the last element of resistance from her mind, leaving her instead to the needs of her poor, starving body which had been denied a man's touch for so long. But there was only one man's touch it craved, and that man had not been there for her.

Until now.

'Tell me,' he urged brokenly. 'For God's sake— tell me!'

'No,' she whispered, and she felt a tear slide beneath her eye. 'Don't go. Stay. Do it. Please, Alexei—'

It was like opening the floodgates—and the strong, dark current of sexual hunger swept him away. He made a noise in the back of his throat which sounded like the triumphant roar of a lion which had gone for its first kill.

With one hand he ripped her panties off and began to caress her, while with the other he pulled distractedly at his leather belt—tossing it over his shoulder. It fell, forgotten, while Victoria writhed beneath the pressure of his fingers as they worked their enchantment.

For a moment he moved away, and her eyes flew open in protest.

'Where are you going?' she questioned, her voice as slurred as if she had drunk a pint of wine.

'I am making myself ready for you.'

She watched him—but it was an odd sensation. Like being a spectator while a film was being run— as if she was part of the action and yet nothing to do with it. But the craving in her body demanded to be fed. She could feel the heavy beat of her blood as it pounded deep in the very cradle of her desire.

Impatiently, he tugged his shirt off, scattering tiny white mother-of-pearl buttons in the process. They clattered and bounced all over the floor. He winced as he unzipped himself, kicking off his trousers and removing his socks until he stood wearing nothing but silk boxer shorts—the hard ridge of him pressing proudly against the soft material, evidence of just how badly he wanted her.

And the shock of seeing *that* again caused a breath of longing to escape from her lips.

'Alexei!' she moaned.

He flicked a glance over at her, and his look of intense concentration became the slow smile of the practised seducer. 'You like me stripping for you, do you, Victoria?'

She swallowed, not secure enough to enjoy it as much as once she could have done. 'Yes.'

Trying to slow the pace down, he slid the boxers off and reached in his pocket for a condom—stroking it onto the steely surface of his erection and almost…almost…

Suddenly he needed her now, and he could not wait. Not for a second, nor even a moment. He couldn't even allow time to remove her dress and her bra, because if he did…

'Victoria.' He groaned as he delved his fingers inside her, feeling her slick heat coating his fingertips and shaking his head, resenting this power she had over him and yet finding it impossible not to yield.

'Victoria…'

This time it was a mixture of plea and protest, but Victoria understood. Even if she hadn't been able to read the signs of desire stretched to breaking-point she had been married to this man, and she knew when his formidable control was slipping…though she had never seen it stretched quite so tightly before.

She reached down and pushed his hand away, and guided him towards her instead—giving a tiny gasp of recognition as she felt the formidable power of him within her grasp once more. She looped her other arm around his neck, drawing his hard, muscular body down on top of hers, and instinct made her lips move gently against his shoulder as her hips rose up to meet him.

'Now,' she urged softly, as his tip pressed against her and a fierce heat began to engulf her. 'Oh, Alexei...now!'

With a moan, he thrust deep inside her—deeper than he had ever been—in her or in any other woman. Deeper even than when he had taken her virginity and she had given it to him so willingly. Something approaching a sob was torn from his throat as he thought of all the men who had been here since him—in this most sacred of places that should have belonged to him and only him. And his moan became angry, his thrust even harder.

'Alexei!' she whimpered, and she could hear the sob of surrender in her own voice.

'I am hurting you?' he demanded.

Not in the way he thought. Her heart was the only threatened casualty. She wanted to put her mouth to his ear and tell him that he was the only man she had ever loved, that even now she sometimes dreamt of him. 'No,' she whispered instead. 'You're not hurting me.'

He saw how close she was, and knew he could not prolong it. Not this time. He lifted her thighs up, putting his arms beneath them so that he could drive into her harder, faster—watching her all the while, watching while her head fell back and her back arched, her legs splaying free of his grasp as her skin began to bloom a soft, deep rose colour before his eyes.

Her cries rang out and Alexei let go—feeling his orgasm take him to a place he'd never visited before. The pleasure felt so sharp, so vivid—it was as though his senses were newly sprung. Even when it had finished he could still feel her violently contracting around him, and he gasped, sinking down on top of her, so that they were all limbs and sighs and meeting, melding flesh. He murmured something in soft Greek against her neck while he grew soft inside her and drifted into oblivion.

Victoria must have fallen asleep, for when she awoke it was to feel the cold marble of the floor cooling the backs of her bare legs, and the sleeping form of Alexei heating her from above as his muscular body covered hers.

But, despite the animal heat of body contact, Victoria shivered a little as she opened her eyes and stared up at the ceiling, trying to keep very still as the memories of what had happened came flooding back, and with them conflicting thoughts which crowded into her mind. She didn't want Alexei to wake. Not yet. Not until she had decided what she was going to do next. But what she needed to do first was accept the situation.

It had happened.

She'd just let her estranged husband make love to her. No, she corrected, painfully but carefully. They had just had wild sex together.

Perhaps it had been inevitable, given their history and the overpowering attraction which had always existed between them. She hadn't planned it, and neither had she prevented it, but she was not going to regret it—no matter how hard she had to try.

Her body felt delicious and heavy, sated with the aftermath of physical pleasure, but inside she was empty. Her lovemaking with Alexei had never been like that before—so mechanical and basic—not even at the end of the marriage. Sex as a cruel imitation of making love—mocking what they had once shared together.

If only it hadn't felt so damned good...

But just as a dreamy smile of memory began to nudge at the corners of her lips she forced herself to remember Alexei's dreadful proposition—that he would pay her to become his mistress, write her a cheque as a divorce settlement.

Treating her like a whore! And she *allowing* herself to be treated like a whore!

Letting him walk right into her suite and have sex with her without putting up any resistance at all. For someone who had objected so violently to his proposition she had certainly had a fast change of opinion.

How *could* she?

She glared at.the ornate chandelier which hung over them like a guillotine.

But she hadn't agreed to become his mistress, had she? Admittedly, they'd had just had sex—but that had happened because… Well, call it a spur-of-the-moment thing that she'd just given in to.

And, while there might have been no softness from Alexei, Victoria had certainly felt tenderness towards *him* when he had been deep inside her—no matter how misplaced it might have been. Some things you just couldn't help—it was as if you were programmed to react in a certain kind of way with certain people. She had slipped into tenderness as easily as slipping on a cashmere sweater on a cold winter's day.

But there had been no bargaining between them. No deal had been struck. She could hold her head up—even though she wasn't particularly proud of what had taken place. It had happened for all kinds of reasons. Oh, for lust—certainly. Especially on Alexei's part. And on her own, too—if she was being completely honest.

Yet it had been about more than lust. It had been

about memory and longing and a need to feel her husband one last time. To remember just how good it could be between them.

But it was over. Victoria knew that, and now she had to think about extricating herself from this potentially embarrassing situation.

Her mind went into overdrive.

Soon he would wake up, and then she would tell him that she wanted to spend the night alone and would prefer it if he left. He had got what he wanted, and if he knew that she wasn't going to agree to a repeat performance then what would be the point in him staying?

Which meant that in the morning she could slip out of here and go straight to the airport.

Why, she'd be on a flight to London before Alexei had even stirred in his luxury Athens apartment!

And she would get by. Somehow. She would manage to pay Caroline everything she owed without asking Alexei for any favours—even if it meant working every hour that God sent to bring in some extra money. The hard work would keep her mind off her own problems—help her forget what had happened here.

Victoria stilled as she felt the body above hers begin to stir, and she hastily closed her eyes, playing for time.

For a split-second Alexei thought it was just a

woman—any woman. Half-asleep, he felt the warm, hard lure of his arousal growing against her sticky heat and made a provocative little thrust.

And then he remembered.

Victoria!

It was as if someone had put his feelings on a merry-go-round and then spun it uncontrollably. He had just done something he had thought was off his agenda for ever—and yet where was the loud, iron clang of closure? Where had his habitual icy control fled to? It had happened without him having a chance to dictate his terms and, unusually, he felt at a disadvantage.

So what now? He knew she was awake—he could feel her holding her breath and then trying to expel it in the slow and controlled way that people did when they were pretending to be asleep.

The subterfuge irritated him as much as his own momentary confusion, and he rolled off her—unwilling to share with her the hard evidence of how quickly she could turn him on. Instead, he leaned on his elbow to survey her ravaged appearance—his black eyes watchful and judgemental. Her dress had ridden up over her hips and her ripped panties lay in a discarded muddle on the floor. Wild hair spilled down over her flushed neck, and her lips were a deep, kiss-bruised scarlet.

Her pretending abandoned, she opened her big blue eyes and looked back at him warily. Like a small animal who had stumbled upon a new and deadly predator and hadn't quite worked out how best to escape.

His irritation grew. Where was her kiss? The soft words of gratitude murmured against his neck? The hand reaching down between his legs to tantalise him all over again?

'You say nothing, Victoria,' he observed evenly. 'Which seems *paraksenos*—strange—given the circumstances.'

Fractionally, she moved away from him—away from the heady danger of his proximity. 'None of the normal reactions seem appropriate in a situation like this,' she said carefully.

'No, *Darling, it was wonderful*?' he mocked.

'You know it was.' On one level.

'Well, what do you *usually* say to men in a *situation like this*?' he mocked. 'What *is* your normal reaction?'

She flushed. His words were no doubt deliberately designed to make her feel like a tramp, and they had succeeded—but she was damned if she was going to tell him. To feed his already over-inflated ego. 'I really don't think that's any of your business,' she answered quietly. 'Do you?'

And—although he told himself it was irrational—Alexei felt a great acrid wave of jealousy engulf him. It didn't matter that they were separated—or that the lawyers would now be engaged in their costly battle. Until the decree absolute was cleared through the cold arena of the court she was still his wife, damn her! Still *his*, and only his.

Black eyes burned into her and he felt a primitive need to demonstrate his power over her. He put his hand down between her legs and touched the precise spot which he knew would make her squirm.

'Alexei!' she gasped.

'Do you like that?' he drawled.

'Y… You know I do.'

He withdrew his fingers and saw the agonised frustration in her eyes. 'Shall I tell you something, Victoria?' he asked softly

'W-what?' She just wanted him to carry on doing what he had been doing, but she was damned if she was going to ask him.

'In future, you really ought to negotiate your price *before* you deliver the goods.' He gave a cruel smile. 'That's the first rule of business.'

It took several seconds for the meaning of his words to register, and when they did they left her in no doubt where she stood. Or who she was. His mistress. His whore. When once she had been the love of his life. She sucked in a shuddering breath, knowing that she must have been mad to have gone into his arms, yet knowing that he was near irre-sistible. She should have pushed him and his black heart as far away from her as was humanly possible.

Her face flushed with an anger which melted

away the last of her tenderness, she wriggled away from him. 'Get out.'

Alexei frowned. 'But I thought we had a deal?'

'Well, you thought wrong.'

'What was that all about, then?'

'A mistake, not a deal,' she said tightly. 'I would rather do a deal with the devil—not that there's much difference between you!'

He played his ace card. 'So suddenly you no longer need the money?'

His smug assumption that she would crumble made Victoria continue to defy him—and to hell with the consequences. 'Not that badly,' she snapped. 'I would rather scrub floors than be under any obligation to you! Now, get out.'

CHAPTER SEVEN

AFTER washing every trace of Alexei from her body, Victoria spent the night curled fitfully in the middle of the vast bed—trying to rid her mind of what they had just done. But the night left her vulnerable, and it was impossible not to re-run the erotic images— like a film she was frightened to watch but unable to tear her eyes away from.

Victoria lay watching the sun rise over Athens with an unbearable sense of sadness. But, after breakfast in her suite—a platter of fruit, thick yoghurt and flower-scented honey—she started to feel human again. The important thing was to try to forget him, and move on. Transfixed by the blue of the Aegean, she was standing on the balcony of her terrace saying a silent farewell to the city when her mobile rang. And she could do absolutely nothing about the answering lurch of her heart—because she knew exactly who it would be.

Alexei!

She put down her coffee cup.

She would tell him that she had absolutely no intention of changing her mind. No matter what he said—and no matter how tempted she was—she would say no.

But it was not Alexei's name which flashed up on the screen, it was Caroline's—and Victoria pressed the button with a frown of confusion.

'Hi, Caro—is everything okay?'

There was a pause. 'Well, that depends on your definition.'

'Nothing's the matter with Thomas?' asked Victoria quickly.

'No, Thomas is fine, but…'

The story came tumbling out. Caroline's understanding landlord was no longer being Mr Nice-Guy. His patience had run out and he wanted his rent money. Preferably the day before yesterday. Or sooner, if that could be arranged.

Victoria stared out at the cloudless sky. She was a businesswoman herself and—even though she wasn't a particularly good one—she couldn't blame the man for claiming what was rightfully his.

'So what did Alexei say?' prompted Caroline eagerly. 'Is he going to give you the money? Was he reasonable?'

Reasonable wasn't a description she had *ever* applied to her husband, and Victoria opened her mouth to say so, then shut it again. What would she say? That Alexei had no intention of giving her anything at all within the time-frame she wanted—not without exacting a sensual payment in kind. And that she'd told him to go to hell. But not to worry because she'd get the money somewhere else.

Well, where?

Even if she waitressed, cooked for mass functions and spent her spare time crafting cakes Victoria was never going to earn enough to pay the backlog of what she owed Caroline to get her landlord off her back. And in the meantime her debts would still be mounting. And Caroline had a child to feed.

'So?' said Caroline, her voice cutting into Victoria's troubled thoughts. 'Did he agree a settlement?'

Victoria closed her eyes. She had already had sex with him and thoroughly enjoyed it—so where was the big sacrifice? Because if she was holding out for the sake of her pride then hadn't he already trampled over it?

'Yes,' she said heavily. 'He's agreed a settlement. But I'm probably going to have to spend a few days here in Athens, hammering it out.'

The irony of her words didn't escape her.

She terminated the connection with Caroline and punched out his number before she had a chance to change her mind.

'*Ne?*'

'Alexei, it's me.'

He had known that, of course. 'Hello, Victoria,' he said softly.

'You're supposed to say, *This is a surprise.*'

'Then I'd be lying. I've been lying here waiting for your call.'

'You were so sure I'd be unable to resist you?'

'Well, you've managed to resist me for seven years,' he said sardonically. 'I imagine that my money has more pulling power.'

She felt stung to defend herself—until she remembered that this wasn't about attempting to rehabilitate her reputation, or telling him that his perception of events was warped. Why cloud the waters any more? Their marriage was coming to an end and it was complicated enough—why complicate it further with needless explanations?

This whole deal would only work if she kept her emotions out of it. If he thought of her as a greedy little gold-digger who wanted to extract the best price for having been married to one of the world's richest men, then let him!

That way, it would be purely functional. He would be as unlike the Alexei of yesteryear as it was possible to be—and surely that would help remove his indelible impression from her heart?

'Hadn't we better talk terms?' she asked calmly.

He'd been expecting passion or sulky resignation—not a cool, practical question—and Alexei was taken off guard. For a moment he wanted to tell her to go to hell—that she was a cold-blooded, avaricious little witch and that his misjudgement of her had been even worse than he'd originally thought.

But surely that would defeat the object of the affair?

Hadn't she haunted his blood for too long—like some lingering and debilitating poison he could never quite rid himself of? So that no matter how enjoyable his sexual experiences they never quite matched up to the memory of Victoria. She was like an erotic ghost who haunted the periphery of every sensual encounter he had.

It was time to bury the myth of her sensuality—to live out every fantasy he'd nurtured since they'd split. And in so doing excise any remaining hold she had over him. Because everyone knew that fantasies were more powerful than reality.

'Certainly we can talk terms,' he agreed, equally coolly. 'Firstly, the liaison will last seven days.'

She closed her eyes. Could she bear it? 'Very well.'

'And during that time you will behave exactly as a mistress should behave.'

An unwelcome arrow of jealousy shafted through her. How many mistresses had he had? 'You mean there's a code of conduct?' asked Victoria furiously.

He heard the note which had sharpened her voice and, correctly assessing its cause, gave a slow smile of satisfaction. 'Of course there is. Mistresses exist to please their masters. They are compliant. They enjoy sex, and agree to it whenever and wherever it is required.'

I can't go through with this!

'So what does that mean in practical terms?' she questioned tonelessly.

He felt the slow beat of anticipation. 'You will wear what pleases me at all times, and you will allow me to dress you. Or undress you. There will be no meaningless stabs at stubborn pride—for I will not have you accompanying me wearing the kind of dress you were wearing at dinner last night.'

'I'm sorry it wasn't expensive enough for your tastes!'

His eyes narrowed as he heard the more accustomed fire in her voice, and he wanted to say, *I like you better when you're feisty*—but again that would be defeating the objective. He didn't want to like her at all.

'My reputation will not be enhanced if you look cheap.'

'In that case I won't unpack my white stilettos!'

'Oh, please do,' he parried softly. 'But save them for bedtime.'

It was a glimpse of the old Alexei and it was terrifying—terrifying because it reminded Victoria of just why she had fallen in love with him. Not just because his stunning good looks made her go weak at the knees and because he was strong and forthright—but because he was funny, too. And in the battle of the sexes every woman knew that laughter was one of the most powerful weapons in a man's armoury.

'Very funny,' she said repressively.

'You will also not—under any circumstances—talk to the press about this arrangement.' His voice had a sudden steely ring to it. 'There will be no story—not now and not ever.'

Her mouth trembled. 'You really think I'd stoop so low as to sell my story to the papers?'

There was a pause. 'Why not? You've already proved you'll do pretty much anything for money.'

It was the most damning assessment he could have given, but in a way his cruel and inaccurate judgement helped her. How much easier to keep her misplaced but volatile emotions out of it if the man she was dealing with blatantly thought so little of her. Genuine gold-diggers must have a really tough time of it, thought Victoria fleetingly. 'So, is that the conclusion of your terms?'

'*Ne,*' he agreed, staring ruefully at the hard rock of his erection outlined beneath the Egyptian cotton sheet and wishing she would get round here so that he could do something with it. 'It is.'

'Then perhaps you'd like to agree to *mine*!'

Alexei's dark brows knitted together in a frown. 'Which are…?'

'I don't want you talking about this either,' she said fervently. 'Not to your friends, your family—no one. Please.'

'You think that I gossip?' he demanded. 'That I should wish to boast of such a conquest?'

'I don't know.'

'You offend my reputation!'

'Just as you have offended mine with your insulting offer!' she stormed back.

There was a pause, and then he started to laugh. 'Oh, very clever, Victoria,' he said softly. 'Very clever indeed. Did you deliberately goad me in order to get me to withdraw?' He gave a soft laugh. 'In a manner of speaking, of course.'

'Don't be so crude!'

'You weren't complaining about that last night!' he threw back at her. 'And I will not change my mind about this settlement—believe me.' Yet the exchange made him wary. It made him realise that— unlike the many women before or since—Victoria had always been able to stimulate a very particular area of his body.

His mind.

Well, his mind was superfluous to requirements…

'There's one more thing.' Victoria drew a deep breath as she remembered the worry she had heard in Caroline's voice. 'I'd like some money up front please.'

'Up front?' he repeated incredulously.

She was going to have to brazen this out—otherwise it simply would not work. 'Let's call it a payment for what happened here last night.'

'*Theos,*' he breathed, his voice shuddering in distaste. 'You pick up the habits of a whore with insulting ease.'

Victoria closed her eyes tightly and prayed for the strength to see this through. 'We have a deal, Alexei,' she said coldly. 'Just stick to your side of it, will you? I would like two thousands pounds—in cash.'

'You think it was worth that much?'

'I think it was worth a damned sight more,' she said truthfully—for if relinquishing all her pride and her values had a price then surely it was more than two thousand pounds.

'I shall have it sent over immediately. Then my car will bring you to meet me—and you can start earning the second instalment.'

For a moment Victoria felt sick. His insults were one thing, but the speed of his arrangements were daunting, with little or no time to prepare herself for what she had now formally agreed to.

'When?' she questioned, suddenly nervous.

'Right now.'

'N-now?' she echoed in alarm, feeling like the condemned man whose execution had just been brought forward.

'I see no point in waiting…in prolonging the anticipation any further, do you?'

What choice did she have?

'Very well,' she agreed weakly.

When the driver arrived she took the money from

him with trembling fingers and instructed the hotel manager's secretary to cable it directly to Caroline in England, who was expecting it. Only when the transaction was completed could Victoria begin to relax—but her journey was all too short as the sleek car whisked her to the other side of the city, and her nerves set in again.

The hotel Alexei had chosen was a tall, gleaming tower set in lovingly tended and watered gardens which were bright with coloured exotic blooms. Inside, the light was muted and dim and welcoming after the glare of the sun—Victoria could see what Alexei had meant about it being discreet, for there were no signs of other guests.

A uniformed guard took her up in a swift and silent lift and Alexei answered the door himself. But for a moment he did not move, not even once the guard had gone. Just stood there as if he had all the time in the world, his gaze drinking her in with anticipation and undisguised triumph.

He was dressed casually. Jeans with the top button carelessly left undone to show a flash of dark, flat belly. Over the top he wore a fine white shirt of silk—and through it Victoria could see the definition of hard muscle and the dark hint of hair-roughened surface.

'You have kept me waiting,' he observed slowly.

Victoria guessed she probably had, by the time she had fussed about with Caroline's money. 'But the best things in life are worth waiting for.' She gave him a cool smile. 'Aren't you supposed to invite me in?'

'I might have other plans in mind,' he murmured. 'I might wish to ravish you on the doorstep.'

Her pulse leapt in response but her smile stayed put. 'Is that really such a good idea?' she questioned in her calmest voice. 'One of the other guests might come and catch you.'

'Other guests?' The black eyes glittered and he gave a low laugh. 'There are no other guests on this floor, *agape*. This part of the building is all mine. No one will disturb us, so you are safe. Now, come here and kiss me.'

Safe was the last thing she felt—even if the suite's very exclusivity hadn't slammed home the huge differences in their status. And she had to stand firm on issues such as Alexei clicking his fingers and expecting her to do his every bidding.

Having sex with him was one thing, but kissing was too intimate—too much a part of their past, when they'd shared *real* kisses. If she refused point-blank to touch her lips to his, then competitive and demanding Alexei would simply see it as a challenge to be overcome—and Victoria had no doubts that he would succeed. No, it would have to be more subtle than that. She would have to avoid intimacy rather than refuse it. She would have to distract him instead.

Flicking her hair back over her shoulders in a shimmering blonde curtain with a deliberately provocative movement, Victoria slanted her estranged husband a smile. 'Let's go inside first, shall we?' she murmured.

But Alexei was watching her as carefully as a jungle predator might observe his prey, and while he silently registered her evasive tactic he did not attempt to dissuade her. His expression was thoughtful as he watched her stroll through the door as if she owned the place—her perfect buttocks thrusting against the cotton of her little dress. Was she simply demonstrating that she would maintain *some* of her independence this week? Or letting him know that actually she *did* have some claim to his property?

For the first time it occurred to him that it was as much in *his* interests to wind up this settlement as quickly as possible as hers. If she suddenly developed a taste for the high life and realised what she had been missing out on she might decide that her initial request had been too modest.

What if she realised during the next week that a halfway decent lawyer would urge her to go for half of everything? But she'll never be able to afford a lawyer that ruthless, he thought with satisfaction.

But Alexei knew enough about human nature to be aware that he must not show any sign of his misgivings. If she suspected that he had the slightest chink in his armour, then she would pounce—and bleed him of every euro she could. And pride would not allow a woman who had betrayed him to compound the damage by fleecing him of his fortune.

He must be very careful not to let the lure of her body blind him the reality of what this arrangement was all about...

He watched as she swiftly glanced around his rooms and already he could feel the hot burn of desire which made him so hard for her. Why? Why so strong and so clamouring with her, always her and only her?

Today, the dress against which her bottom thrust so delectably was pure white—and few women in their twenties would have been able to wear such an unstructured little garment successfully. But Victoria could. She knew the most fundamental rule of fashion—that it was the body which counted, and if your body was good enough you could wear rags and make them look like couture.

'You come to me all in white, dressed like the bride you once were?' he mused. 'My little virgin!'

Victoria's heart was pounding so hard that it hurt. The starter's gun had been fired and they were off—and the concept of what was about to happen was only just beginning to dawn on her. 'Except that I'm not a virgin.'

'No. Not this time. Not like the first time. Ah—what pleasure that gave me!'

The appeal that widened her blue eyes was genuine. 'Alexei—must we?'

'Must we what?' he questioned disingenuously. 'This is a unique situation—surely you wish to explore it?'

'No! That's the last thing I want!'

'Well, I *do*,' he said flatly, in a tone of voice which emphasised that *he* was calling the tune. He saw the slump of resignation replace the apprehension in her tense shoulders and, strangely, this did not please him either. He felt as if he were about to begin a long, hard race in arduous conditions—but that even victory would not bring him relief.

'Tell me, *oreos*, did it feel different last night?'

'Different to what?' she questioned tonelessly—wondering how she could have thought that this ordeal was only to be about sex. This seemed to be more about power.

'To the others, of course!' His breathing was laboured and it felt as if he was driving a stake of steel through his own chest. Because—no matter what his feelings for Victoria were today—he could not rid himself of the primitive but very real belief that she was his. His wife. His possession. Not for very much longer, but until then…yes. *His*. And only his.

'What are you t-talking about,' she said, shaken by the venom in his voice.

'The other men,' he elaborated, and when he saw

the colour drain from her face he doubled the amount of lovers he had mentally calculated that she must have worked her way through. 'The ones who have been with you since our marriage ended. How did they feel when compared to me? Was it better? Different? Did they feel as good inside you? As big? Did they make you come as many times as I do, Victoria?'

'Stop it!' She clapped her hands over her ears and closed her eyes, and when she opened them again it was to see him surveying her closely. Almost as if he had overstepped the mark...

But he hadn't. She had come this far, and in a way having to swallow her pride and agree to his monstrous suggestion had been the biggest hurdle. Nothing worse could happen now, surely? Judging by last night, the sex, she knew, would be terrific. If she could just withstand the cruel lash of his tongue, then she would survive this. She had to. For Caroline and Thomas's sake—but most of all for her own.

Fight back, she urged herself. Fight him on the same territory—for you have nothing to lose.

'And what about you?' she questioned acidly. 'All the women who followed me—how did it feel with them? Was it as good?'

His eyes narrowed. 'You really want me to tell you?'

Swiftly, she walked over to the window, staring

blindly out at the view—but at least he wouldn't be able to detect her sudden vulnerability or see the sudden pricking of tears in her eyes. 'No.' Composing herself, she turned back again. 'No, I don't.'

But was he going to taunt her with his fevered imaginings all week? And was she going to let him? Bad enough that he considered he had bought her for a week—but to have that compounded by his jealous and unfounded accusations would surely make an intolerable situation even worse.

And suddenly she found herself saying, 'There hasn't been another man, Alexei.'

Her stark words seemed to tumble out of the air like rocks brought down from a cliff-face by a violent storm. He stared at her as they hit him. 'You lie!' he breathed.

'But that is where you are wrong!' Her eyes lit with a challenge. 'You're the only man I've ever had sex with. My first and only lover.'

'And what of the man I discovered you with after you left Greece?'

'You know damned well that nothing happened with Jonathan!'

'Jonathan?' he mocked viciously. 'You think I am blind? I know what I saw!'

Even now he could remember the savage white rage which had burned through him. That devastating moment of uncertainty—of wondering whether she had cheated on him. As a man who had never known an atom of doubt, he had found those dark, nebulous fears intolerable. For the first and only time in his life he had felt vulnerable, and he had decided that if that was what relationships could do for you, then he wanted out. And, in a way, hadn't he spent the intervening years running from that unbearable hurt?

'I know how it must have looked, and I'm... sorry.' Seeing him start to speak, Victoria held up her hand—like a judge commanding a court to be silent. There was an incredulous flare of answering light in his black eyes. 'Please, Alexei—just let me please say this. I need to tell you how it was.'

She drew a deep breath, wanting to choose her words carefully, realising that was putting herself in the precarious position of laying herself open to him and making herself vulnerable in the bargain. And yet she had to try—because anything had to be better than being misjudged by him.

'You were never there for me in Greece.'

'So you ran away?' he accused quietly.

Had she? The relationship hadn't been working, true—but she had contributed to its demise, she recognised now. She should have stayed. Fought harder to put things right between them instead of just letting things slide and then putting herself in a compromising position by staying with another man.

At the time she had told herself that if Alexei was

so quick to believe her capable of infidelity then the kind of trust on which secure marriages flourished had been lacking right from the start. It was only time which had thrown a different perspective on things.

'Maybe I did,' she admitted. 'But I just couldn't see any other way out. My trip to England was never meant to be anything other than a temporary escape—it just snowballed. But I swear *on my life*, Alexei, that there was never any of the kind of intimacy you imagined with Jonathan.'

'But it was still intimate. You know it was. You were sharing the kind of closeness which should have been reserved for me,' he said darkly, his voice obdurate, his eyes narrowing. 'And why did you tell me nothing of this at the time?'

'Because after you stormed off you wouldn't take my phone calls! All my letters were returned unopened! I tried and tried to get in touch with you.' Her eyes met his in a candid stare. 'Or are you denying knowledge of all that?'

There was a long silence. 'No.' He had believed her to be guilty—in all his youth and passion unable to conceive that a man could live with his beautiful Victoria and not want to bed her. By the time he had calmed down enough to consider hearing her explanation the letters and the phone calls had stopped. It had seemed that she'd given up—and maybe that in itself had been an admission of guilt.

Or at least that was what he had allowed himself to believe—for his own pride had prevented him from getting on a plane to talk to her about it. And the hurt and confusion had shaken a man who had always considered himself strong. The downside to love was too high a price to pay, he had decided.

Victoria shook her head. 'Oh, what's the point in analysing it?' she questioned bitterly. 'It's all past. Done.' Wrecked and ruined... Suddenly an overwhelming wave of sadness and regret washed over her.

Alexei sighed. Had he thought this would be easy? As easy as it had been last night, when he had just taken her in his arms and plundered what was still rightfully his? She had just made it *ena ekatomirio* times harder. Her eyes were clouded and her face etched with pain, but he closed his mind and his heart to it and concentrated on his sexual hunger instead. Perhaps this was the way it worked best. No talk. No memories. Just this...

'Come here,' he instructed softly.

Power. Always power. *Don't make me. Please don't make me.*

'Alexei...'

'I said come here,' he repeated silkily.

'I c-can't move.' And it was true—her legs felt as if they were rooted to the spot, as if someone had poured concrete over her feet and let it dry.

Alexei, too, was turned to stone by the full power

of his arousal. And daunted by its intensity. Damn her—*damn her*! But someone had to break the deadlock before it became unbreakable, and he moved to her with the exquisite awkwardness of a schoolboy. 'You want that we play games?' he demanded, his usual effortless fluency deserting him.

And although she could see torment on his face Victoria knew that it was merely sexual frustration. She also knew that she was susceptible to a whole lot more than that. And that every time she exposed herself to intimacy with Alexei she ran the risk of being hurt. Had she thought that after her admitting there had been no other lover he would show mercy to her? Let her go quietly, settlement in hand and no price to pay? Because, if so, she had made a serious error of judgement.

'Are you out of your mind?' she demanded. 'This *whole charade* is one *big* game—or do you live your life like this, Alexei? In this unreal world of subterfuge and bargaining?'

Without intending to do so, he suddenly lifted his fingertips to her cheek and brushed them against its velvet smoothness. 'Right now, this feels more real than the ground beneath my feet,' he said simply.

The words took her by surprise, and Victoria found herself captivated by them as surely as if they had been made of silken mesh to bind her to him. Her breath caught in her throat as his hands caught her waist, lifting her towards him as if she had been made of cotton wool. And that, too, was irresistible—for she wasn't a fragile little thing, and for a man to make her feel tiny and helpless was quite some feat.

And if a fragment of her mind niggled away to tell her that this was all to do with control, she ignored it—meeting his questioning gaze as he lowered her back down to the ground, this time close enough for their bodies to brush.

He wanted to kiss her—badly—but kissing seemed inappropriate somehow, and she had avoided it earlier. The ice needed to be broken—the deal set in motion without further confrontation. 'Victoria,' he said softly, lacing his fingers in between his. 'Come.'

He led her into the vast bedroom like a sacrificial lamb—but Victoria was aware of the excited beat of her heart and knew that she could be no hypocrite. This might all be wrong, but she wanted Alexei just as badly as he professed to want her.

'Look out over the city,' he whispered, pointing to the window. 'My city.'

Glad for the momentary reprieve from his touch, which was sending her emotions haywire, Victoria looked out at the rooftops. They gleamed in the bright sunshine—each one representing its own closed little world. Just as up here—for now at least-they were in their own world, too.

'Are we staying here?' she questioned, because

somehow it was easier to ask the big things when she didn't have to look into that glittering ebony stare. Because that was the trouble. His eyes looked the same, when things were not the same. Everything had changed, to become a travesty of what had taken place between them before—and if Victoria wanted to emerge from this with her sanity intact she would do well to remember that.

'Certainly for the next couple of hours,' came his sardonic reply.

Victoria flicked her tongue over her lips. 'That wasn't what I meant.'

'No. I know it wasn't. You want a detailed itinerary of the week to come?'

'Just some idea.'

'I thought that we could have a little…variety.' He moved behind her and began to kiss the back of her neck, his hands reaching up to cover the breasts which peaked against his palms, and her knees sagged as she leaned against him. 'You like variety, don't you, Victoria?'

'Alexei!' She shuddered and closed her eyes.

'So, shall we go somewhere different for dinner tonight?'

Anywhere. 'Where?'

'Paris?'

'*P-Paris?*'

'*Ne.* Why not? Somewhere away from my home city—from a place which might *inhibit* me.'

The innuendo was accompanied by a blatant thrust of his hardness against the mound of her bottom, and Victoria couldn't prevent herself from moaning his name.

'Alexei!'

'You wouldn't like me to be inhibited, would you, Victoria?'

Quite honestly, she felt so dazed that if he'd suggested they rough it on the streets of Athens she would have agreed to it. Anything. As long as he didn't stop touching her where he was touching her… But his fingers had stilled as he waited for an answer, and even though some distant part of her despised the ease with which he could seduce her, her greedy body would not let her resist. 'No,' she agreed on a shaky note. 'Of course I wouldn't.'

Alexei felt a surge of mastery and of need—and a determination to remain more in control this time. Last night he had been a man satisfying his hunger with an almost savage appetite—and he had shown Victoria that she still exerted a power over him. And that was dangerous. Very dangerous.

So today he would take it slowly. He would drive her mad with wanting as he prepared to savour the feast.

'I have a few people to see while we're there— and you can hit the shops.' He gave her a benign smile. 'Paris is the best place in the world for clothes. Or so I'm told—is that true?'

She wanted to demand to know who had told him—but suspected that the answer would hurt her. And why the hell was she starting to feel jealous over a man from whom she couldn't wait to be legally free? 'I wouldn't know,' she answered coolly.

'Then you must allow me to educate you,' came his silky response.

If his intention had been to rub in the fact that he was paying and she was being bought, then he had more than succeeded. And if it hadn't been for the debt owed and the promise made to her best friend she would have dragged herself away from the temptation of his touch—no matter how much her body screamed out its protest.

He didn't just inhabit a different world—Alexei was so wealthy that it was almost as if he was living in a parallel universe. But in a funny kind of way didn't it reassure her to acknowledge the differences between them? To know that it could never have worked. Never.

'You're just too kind,' she said sardonically.

He smiled. 'Aren't I just?'

Tiptoeing his fingers over her pale skin, Alexei slid the zip of her dress down so that it pooled at her feet, then lifted her out of it. Soon she would be wearing clothes more worthy of her beauty—he would bestow on her all the costly gowns the great fashion houses had to offer. Unashamedly, he would seduce her with them.

And afterwards she would take them back to England with her—where they would look as out of place as strands of spun gold dropped in among a bale of straw. But the riches would remind her...would taunt her with the knowledge of the kind of life she could have lived but had chosen to forego. Let her see for herself what a fool she had been!

His bitter thoughts only fed his desire.

'Come to bed,' he said harshly, and it was with a grim smile of anticipation that he picked up the half-clothed body of his estranged wife and carried her over to the vast double bed.

CHAPTER EIGHT

VICTORIA had only ever had a brief taste of Alexei's wealth—and then it had not really felt like his, except by proxy. Back then he had not had control of the Christou billions, but now he did. Quickly she became aware of how important a figure he had become, and what a powerful role he occupied on the world stage of big business.

He had a fleet of aircraft rather as a small boy might keep toy cars in a garage. There was a jet big enough to fly the Atlantic, there were helicopters, and a smaller aircraft which could land on the tiny runways at Aspen and the numerous private airfields of Europe.

Suddenly she was seeing a different side of the man she had married. When they'd met he had been barely out of studenthood, and he had taken her to live in the house of his parents. Although his wealth had been there—it had always been hovering in the background.

But, oh, how things had changed.

He flew her to Paris, where a car was waiting to take them to one of the French capital's most famous hotels.

'You don't have your own apartment in Paris?' questioned Victoria in surprise, as they walked into the sumptuous lobby.

Was she taking an inventory? Alexei wondered. Upping her claim on his fortune second by second? 'Of course I do,' he answered smoothly. 'But on this occasion I prefer the relative anonymity of a hotel.

Their hotel was situated just off the Champs Élysées, with no great fanfare announcing it—just restrained luxury and the most discreet of staff. Inside, tiny lights glimmered in the perfectly shaped box trees which lined the foyer and their suite was lavish—though only slightly more lavish than the one she'd stayed in at Athens.

Victoria had been expecting Alexei to take her clothes off straight away—and it was pointless to resent the fact that she wanted that more than anything. But he threw his jacket down, loosened his shirt collar and took out his mobile phone.

'First I have to make a couple of calls,' he explained, and, seeing her expression, he shrugged and answered her unspoken question. 'No, I *can't* get out of them.' His smile was slow, his voice lowering into a note of velvet promise. 'But I've arranged for someone to bring over a dress for you to wear to dinner tonight. You can have the run of the shops tomorrow!' There was a speculative glitter in his eyes. 'Come and show me when you're wearing it,' he added, heading towards the bedroom just as there was a knock at the door. He turned back. 'And don't be long.'

Victoria felt like a little girl who had been told to run away and dress up. She had never had anyone 'bring over a dress' before, and felt vaguely out of her depth. But the stylist spoke English with a charming French accent and was both delightful and diplomatic.

'I bring you something I think Monsieur Christou will like.' She smiled conspiratorially as she carefully took out a gown and began to unpack flimsy underwear from between layers of tissue paper. 'I thought this one would be *parfait pour ce soir, mademoiselle*. You like to try it so that I can check for size?'

Victoria smiled at the stylist, telling herself that the woman was only doing her job. She stared at the gown—which was bright red and showy, in a colour and design she would never normally have chosen. Lying on the bed was matching underwear—an outrageous balcony bra, a skimpy little thong, and a *frou-frou* of a suspender belt to clasp silk stockings as fine as gossamer.

Victoria supposed that some women might feel as if they had opened up a bottomless treasure chest, but for her it seemed…tainted. Did the stylist provide this kind of service for Alexei's women regularly? she wondered, as she slithered into the underwear and then shoehorned her way into the scarlet lace dress

Why, she looked as if she should be touting for trade along the Pigalle!

She tottered into the bedroom on spindly red heels and Alexei—who had been talking animatedly on the phone in Greek—turned round, his appreciative smile fading when he saw her expression. He said something terse and then severed the connection.

There was something in his black eyes which Victoria didn't recognise, something she didn't like, and suddenly she realised that anyone could make a deal in theory—could decide that sex was just sex and probably the best sex you would ever have in your life. You could tell yourself that it was worth it for the money you'd be getting—and that you needed it very badly for your friend. You could even try telling yourself that you were having sex with your ex so it was no big deal.

So why did she suddenly feel sordid? Cheap? As if she'd *sold* herself? Because she had! And because reality was a million miles away from fantasy, and suddenly being his mistress left a sour taste in her mouth. Suddenly she wanted to be his wife again.

'Victoria?' he questioned. 'What is it?'

Frustrated and angry, she yanked off one of the high-heeled shoes and hurled it at the wall.

Bemused, Alexei watched while the second one followed it with a loud thud. Then she reached for her zip and yanked it down, before peeling the dress from her delectable body and throwing it at him.

He caught it and flourished the scarlet scrap of lace like a bullfighter. 'As a striptease it leaves a little to be desired,' he commented wryly.

'It wasn't designed to provoke—I just couldn't wait to get it off my back.'

A pulse worked in his cheek. 'You want me that badly?'

'Oh, please don't insult my intelligence!'

'You don't like the colour?'

'I hate it! It makes me look like a tart!'

But Alexei shook his head and dropped the dress on the bed, moving towards her with stealth and purpose. 'On the contrary—it makes you look extremely beautiful. A grown-up. A woman. Dressed as a woman should be dressed. In the finest clothes that money can buy.'

But Victoria felt sick. The disparity between their worlds was more than disturbing. She had felt better about herself in her chainstore outfit. 'The amount this cost could feed a family of four for a week!'

'Yet the brief pleasure it gave me was incalculable,' he whispered, pulling her into his arms and drifting his lips over her neck. 'Doesn't that make it worth it?'

She closed her eyes. 'Alexei, stop it.'

He put his hand between the fork of her thighs. 'But you like it,' he murmured. 'You know you do.'

'There is a woman standing patiently waiting next door.'

'Then let her wait!' he said arrogantly.

'No!'

'Yes.' And he drove his mouth down on hers with a ruthless seeking pressure deliberately designed to melt away all her objections with its sheer sensual power.

For a moment Victoria wavered—achingly aware of the expert stroke of his fingers, the way they were igniting the building fire of desire. But with an almighty effort she pulled away from his sweet caress, her breathing ragged and her blue eyes dilated into ebony saucers as she shook her head.

'No!' she cried again.

His eyes narrowed. 'You don't mean that,' he protested, wondering if she knew just how magnificent she looked, striking a pose of defiance in that amazing underwear and managing to look more sexy than any woman he had ever seen. Was this really the shy little girl he had married—the woman whose innocence he had taken?

'Oh, but I do! I am *not* leaving that poor woman standing out there while we get it on in here!'

'I will send her away.'

'You will not!'

'I will do anything I damned well please!'

'Not if you want my co-operation, you won't!'

'We—have—a—deal.' He bit the words out.

'Which does not include embarrassing someone who is only doing her job!'

'And *you* are supposed to be doing *your* job!' he flared. 'You are my mistress!'

'And until the decree absolute comes through I am also still your wife!' she whipped back. 'And as such I deserve some respect! So will you damned well give me some?'

There was a silence punctured only by the fractured sound of their breathing, and suddenly Alexei started to laugh.

Had he thought that she would be some kind of push-over? And wouldn't it have been easier, in a way, if she were? He sighed with a grudging admiration at her defiance.

'Indeed you are my wife.' He nodded, and swallowed down his desire. 'So, is your objection to the clothes on the grounds of cost or because someone else made the choice for you? Perhaps it was both those things?' He saw her hesitation and found himself in the extraordinary position of trying to gauge a woman's mood and to attempt to placate her. But why was he bothering to do that when by rights he should snap his fingers and demand that she give him exactly what he wanted?

Because he realised that he did not want her mood to be flat. He wanted her to be Victoria—with all her captivating and infuriating traits. She had a stubborn and resilient side to her—or else why would she not have come asking for money years ago, when their marriage was still fresh and their emotions raw and the lawyers could have fed off that freshness and pain and made her a fortune?

Wouldn't it be more of an achievement to get her to relax? To coax her into dropping that brittle air? He sucked in a deep breath, justifying it by telling himself that it would make her more amenable to his advances. He felt the sudden wild thumping of his heart, the inexplicable need to see her smile. 'What if I give you one of my credit cards and in the morning you can go and buy what you like?'

Victoria knew that he was offering her an olive branch. He wasn't to know that it offended her pride to be offered a free hand with his plastic—in his macho way he probably thought it was the most wonderful gift he could give a woman. And it *was* a peace offering.

'You would trust me with your credit card?'

'I wouldn't advise you to attempt fraud.' But his voice was soft with humour.

Victoria stared at the lush lines of his mouth, which would soon be kissing the most intimate parts of her body, and she felt the first slow heating of desire. 'H-how much can I possibly wear in a week?'

'But that is the exquisite irony.' He shrugged his broad shoulders and threw her a look of anticipation. 'You wear as little as possible, *agape mou*.'

At least his blatantly sexual words brought her to her senses, for her heart had started to lurch in painful recognition that this arrangement was very definitely finite. Why, she should be ticking off the hours—like a woman in a prison cell. But wasn't it a strange and bitter truth that you could so quickly grow accustomed to the face of a man you had once loved?

And loved still? asked the tormenting voice of her conscience.

No! Sexual desire wasn't love. She pushed the troublesome thoughts away and gave him a noncommital smile. 'So why waste my time buying clothes?'

'So that I can take them off,' he murmured, but he could see he'd hurt her and wished he could undo his words—and so much more besides. For a moment he wanted to pull out the clips which constrained her blonde hair and bury his face in its honeyed tumble. To wipe away the past as if it had never happened.

And then he forced himself to remember the real reason why they were alone in a Paris bedroom.

She wanted money and he wanted sex.

Supply and demand.

Simple.

He allowed his gaze to travel slowly over her as if she were any other woman. It was overtly sensual, and this time bordered on insulting, and he knew it.

But when a woman sold her sexuality for hard cash she forfeited any respect along the way—wife or not. 'So why don't you go and dismiss the stylist— and then return to me so that we can finish this...'

Running a finger slowly and deliberately down over her lace-encased nipple, he felt it peak, and her lips parted instinctively in an unspoken invitation to kiss them. A man could drown in a look like that. With an effort of will he turned away, and the surge of power he felt in resisting that kiss was in itself almost sexual.

'In fact—' his gaze swivelled round to the discarded scarlet dress '—as you now seem to have nothing to wear I suggest we order up Room Service and spend the evening in.' He slid his hand over the curve of her bottom.

She wanted to tell him not to play with her as he would a puppet. Yet the sudden vulnerability she felt inside frightened her far more than his sexual power over her—or the fact that he despised what she was doing. Physically and emotionally she felt pulled this way and that—like a stray leaf being tossed about by a turbulent stream—but the bitter twist was that she felt more *alive* than she'd done in years.

What would he say if she told him that she wished she could cut short their agreement and walk out of here right now?

He would say she was lying.

And, of course, he would be right.

CHAPTER NINE

'ARE we spending our last couple of days here?' Victoria questioned, with just the right amount of casualness in her voice as she traced her finger along Alexei's arm.

They were lying in bed looking at the terracottas and greens of the Florentine skyline and Alexei had been miles away—somewhere oddly peaceful—but he turned now to look at Victoria, thinking how young she looked. Almost as young as when first he had met her. And this was still how he liked her best—stripped of all artifice. Even the fine clothes he had insisted on buying for her paled into insignificance when contrasted with her natural loveliness. Those blue eyes and that perfect skin did not need make-up to define them, and he liked her hair best when it was rumpled and tumbling free.

How poignant it could be—that strange time after orgasm, when his senses felt both raw and yet numbed and his mind played tricks with him. Torturing him with memories of what he'd once had and reminding him that things could never be the same again. And, even if they could, he would not wish them to be. Alexei shut his eyes. Of course he wouldn't.

But things could change inside your head. It was as if his eyes had been opened to see that life around him was changing all the time—and that even the recent past had the power to transform events.

He remembered the tension in Paris after the stylist had left—with Victoria smarting from his cavalier treatment of her. They had gone to bed, both of them simmering with rage—all the ingredients of another cold-hearted yet hot-blooded encounter. But then they had looked deep into the other's eyes and...*vrondi*.

Something had happened—but what?

One of those curious distortions of time—where past and future had dissolved into glorious present. That night they had come together as equals—the bitterness and quarrels forgotten in the sweetness of an embrace which had taken his breath away. As if all the years in between had never happened. She had kissed him properly and he had kissed her back and it had shaken him. Made him feel things he had not wanted or expected to feel.

For an unsentimental man, not given to introspection, he had been made uneasy. Until he'd reminded himself that their lovemaking had always been sensational. It was a powerful physical chemistry—that was all. And that had dampened down his strange sense of disquiet—until now, as her words brought it all flooding back.

'Our last days?' he repeated slowly, and it sounded like a death sentence.

'Well, yes.' Her voice was bright. 'The deal *was* for a week. Remember? And the week is nearly up.'

The deal. Alexei's mouth curved with faint disdain. He *wanted* her to remind him of the money—of what she was prepared to do to get it. Because that was easier than admitting he'd forgotten all about the damned deal.

'So it is,' he murmured, and turned onto his side so that the sheet fell from his dark body, revealing his powerful physique and the unmistakable stirring of arousal. 'So, do you want to spend it here in Florence? Or we could fly to Barcelona if you wish.' His black eyes glittered. 'Or straight back to Athens?'

The choice of cities made Victoria feel dizzy, and yet strangely she wanted to go back to Athens— even though anything to do with Greece had the power to make her feel nostalgic. Just face up to it, she thought. Soon you will be back in England—a richer and wiser woman, ready to put your relationship with Alexei behind you.

'Let's go back to Athens,' she said softly, sliding her hand between his thighs, glad that his eyes fluttered to a close—blinding him to the pain which briefly clouded her face.

*   *   *

The plane took off soon after dawn and he took her back to the tall glass tower set among the lush, tropical plants—kissing her thoroughly in the lift as it rode up to his penthouse, tucking his hand beneath the tiny skirt she wore so that she groaned to the orchestration of his expert touch.

And when he opened the door and they tumbled inside there was no finesse as they fell on each other like two people who hadn't a second to waste. He took her first on the floor, and then carried her to the Jacuzzi and made love to her there, amid the warm, bubbling waters, until she cried out in disbelief that anything could be so perfect.

Afterwards they swam in the private pool, picked at lunch ordered from Room Service, and the afternoon passed with what seemed to Victoria like a virtuoso performance of Alexei's sensual skills.

But her heart was heavy as they drank champagne and decided where to go for dinner. She stared sightlessly at the potted lemon trees which fringed the large terrace and wondered just how they would leave matters between them. Would there be a discussion about the outstanding money he owed her? Or would Alexei just do the honourable thing and present her with a generous cheque? And how would she feel about *that*?

Victoria sighed. In the beginning it hadn't been that difficult to drive a hard bargain, but now the subject of finance seemed oddly out of place. Because you've grown too close to him, she told herself—closer than you ever meant to. You've crossed some invisible line and there's no way of knowing whether you'll ever be able to get back.

Alexei saw the confusion on her face and wondered if her mind was as full of reluctance as his. He smoothed his fingertips over the dewy softness of her skin, feeling the warm flickering of her pulse against the delicate skin at her temple. And suddenly he wanted more.

He took her face between her hands and stared at her for a long time, his eyes seeming to ask all kinds of silent questions before he bent his head to kiss her. It began as a featherlight brush of lips which met and melded until he coaxed hers apart. And then her arms came up around his neck and the kiss became deep and drugging. Alexei could taste wine and chocolate on her mouth, could hear the little sighs of pleasure she made and feel the softness of her breasts against him.

Almost as if everything were happening in a dream he moved over her, silently asking and receiving her wordless assent as she parted her legs for him and he took her in one long, delicious thrust, with her back pressed against the stone flags of the terrace.

He felt her shudder as he entered her—saw her mouth soften and her eyes dilate with pleasure—and he groaned, wanting to prolong it and yet almost not daring to. For something intangible had crept in to complicate the sweetness of what he was doing.

They had not made love like this in years.

'Alexei?' She whispered his name, her voice trembling—because his kiss and his touch had mimicked a long-forgotten tenderness.

'*Kesero*,' he murmured unsteadily.

She knew that meant *I know*—as if he understood—but surely he wasn't experiencing the same as her? This wasn't supposed to happen—and it *isn't* happening, she told herself fiercely. It's all in your love-starved imagination. And then the waves of pleasure starting building.

She could feel the damp heat of his muscular body as he moved within her, and the hard jut of his hips against the soft cushion of hers. Her body stretched into an arc as she ran her fingertips over the smooth curve of his buttocks, the pleasure increasing to an unbearable pitch, finally engulfing her so that she fell over the edge in perfect time with him and shuddered to stillness within the circle of his arms.

Alexei saw the soft shadows which played on her face, and the bright gleam of her eyes as she gave him a tremulous smile. And he knew then that he had not had enough. 'I do not want this to end, Victoria,' he groaned.

'It *is* ending, though—isn't it, Alexei?' she questioned softly.

He shook his dark head, his hand now cupping her chin, so that the waterfall of pale hair spilled all over his fingers in scented, silken waves. 'But there is nothing to stop us carrying on like this, is there?' Because this was perfection, frozen in time. No expectations—and therefore no disappointments. This way it was simple. This way there was no hurt. No broken promises.

Victoria frowned. 'Carrying on like this?' she repeated slowly. 'Like *what*, exactly?'

His black eyes were intent, and glittered like shards of jet. 'Stay here.'

She waited.

'As my mistress.'

Her heart plummeted, even though she kept her face neutral. So that was his offer. More of the same. Just an extension of the original insulting contract. Did he have any idea of how much that hurt, even while—perversely—the thought of leaving him filled her with so much dread that for one mad moment she was even prepared to consider it?

But the offer made her feel like a commodity. Or maybe that was his intention. He had done it before and he was doing it again. Reminding her of her true role in his life and not to get ideas above her station—reinforcing the fact that he was calling all the shots.

But only if she let him.

Yet how could she not, when she still wanted him

so badly? She always had and perhaps she always would—unless she allowed time to come to her rescue, as it surely would. Being a mistress for a week wasn't really long enough for the novelty and the re-ignition of the sexual excitement between them to have faded.

Yet that might happen all on its own if she stayed. Or was she just making excuses—trying to dress up her reasons for remaining when the only reason was that she wanted him so much? Loved him so much, she realised—but her heart clenched with pain and there was no joy in her silent admission.

Because he had hurt her badly, and something made her want to hurt him back. And maybe it was an acid test—to see whether he had one drop of vulnerability coursing around his veins. She stared up into his rugged face with its hard mouth and assessing eyes.

'Just how long did you have in mind?' she questioned lightly, and saw an unmistakable triumph begin to curve his lips.

'We can reassess it in…say…' He shrugged his powerful shoulders. 'A month?'

Was he expecting her to fall to her knees in gratitude? Victoria studied him. Yes, on one level she suspected that he was.

She nodded. 'Very well. I will continue to be your mistress, Alexei,' she said softly. And as she saw his expression begin to relax, she inflicted her own crushing blow. 'But I will never be your wife again.'

There was a stunned silence as he stared at her—his pride wounded and the unbelievable prospect of rejection hovering like a spectre in the shadows. Until his clever mind sifted through the facts.

'I don't remember asking you to be my wife again!' he objected silkily. But curiosity got the better of him and his brows darkened with a slowly dawning and disbelieving rage. 'Why the hell not?'

'You mean, after last time?' She saw the hot, dark fire in his eyes, but she knew she couldn't run away from this. She had to tell him—because up until now they had been poised on the edge of the whole issue of their marriage—like two skaters on a lake, who didn't know how deep the ice went and were scared to put a blade to it.

But sooner or later one of them had to test it out—no matter if it cracked wide open beneath the weight of examination. For didn't they both need to confront the truth of the past, no matter how painful, whatever the consequences? 'Our marriage was a disaster, Alexei. You know it was.'

There was a tense, expectant silence.

'And you're blaming me? Is that it?' he snapped.

She stared at him. 'I'm trying to tell it how it was. Maybe it might have been different if I hadn't had to spend so much time on my own. I was lonely—and it just seemed to get worse and worse.'

'How the hell can you have been lonely?' he demanded. 'You had my parents! My sisters! You were surrounded by people!'

'Who all thought you had married unsuitably! Especially your mother.'

'But you were poor and a foreigner, and we were both too young—that was how they saw it. My family only wanted what was best for me—surely you can understand why my mother wasn't initially overjoyed?'

His brutal honesty took her breath away. He was asking her to rubber-stamp his mother's disapproval of his bride! And yet, in a way, nothing had changed. She was still that girl. Still unsuitable. Still with barely a word of Greek to her name. And even if she *did* become his mistress there was no bright and beautiful future waiting somewhere in the sunset.

'But instead of supporting me, trying to convince your parents that I could be a good wife, you did nothing. You let me get on with it. You left me in Athens while you trotted around the globe.'

'And I was doing that for *us*!' he declared furiously. '*Theos*, Victoria, I was working myself to the ground—it wasn't some kind of extended glorified holiday!'

'But I felt like you'd ditched me—as if I had stepped into a strange half-world of not fitting in, when all my friends were off at uni having a great time.' Looking back, it all seemed as if it should have been manageable, but at the time it had appeared insurmountable. Victoria shrugged awkwardly. 'I was—as you say—very young.'

Alexei shook his dark head in frustration. 'I cannot believe that you are bringing this up now—when it is no longer relevant!'

'You don't think so?'

'No, I do not! I have been more than generous in my offer to make you my mistress.' His mouth curved disdainfully. 'An offer which would make you the envy of every woman in Athens! I was prepared to forgive you for your indiscreet behaviour as my bride. I was even prepared to forgive you for daring to criticise my family—and yet you have thrown it all back in my face with your ungratefulness!'

'*Ungratefulness?*' she choked in disbelief.

'*Ne!* Why don't you stop to think about it for a moment? As I said, the reason I was away so much was because I was working hard—for *us*—not just to prove myself, but also to provide us with our own home. But that never entered your head, did it?'

'And you never stopped for a moment to think what it might be like for me, did you, Alexei? You just expected me to slot into the place in which you'd put me like a new piece of furniture!'

'Now you are being *impossible*!'

'*I'm trying to tell you how it was!*' she pleaded.

'You think that marriages are made in heaven?'

'Certainly not ours! You were so remote, Alexei! I felt as though I was bottom of your list of needs.'

'And you were so demanding!' he returned. 'I was learning how to do business for the first time, and I was having to do it in front of scores of people who would have liked to see the boss's son fail. When I came back all I wanted to do was to wind down, and yet you clung onto me like a limpet to a rock.'

Victoria shook her head in hurt and frustration. Couldn't he see how she'd felt? Obviously not. Her agonies of insecurity which had been exacerbated by her youth and her inexperience? But Alexei wasn't the kind of man who was interested in what a woman was thinking or feeling. A woman's role was to be decorative and to provide sex and that was never going to be enough—not for her.

There was no point in raking over the past. Not any more. Nothing could ever make the relationship what it should have been—and surely this was just prolonging the agony.

She gave a heavy sigh. 'We could stand here and trade insults all day, couldn't we? Or I could do us both a favour and go back to England, where I belong. So I'll decline the chance of being your mistress—thanks all the same, Alexei.'

His eyes narrowed. 'You are *turning me down*?' he demanded incredulously.

Self-preservation gave her no alternative. She could see that his pride and his ego had been wounded by her refusal, and she recognised that it might actually do him a favour. Yet the moment gave her no joy—because it was slowly sinking in that this really *was* goodbye. The door between past and present, which had always been slightly ajar, was now about to be slammed firmly shut.

In a way, hadn't she just made everything worse for herself by coming back? At least in the intervening years she had learnt to live without him—had grown used to a life without passion. But now Alexei had reawakened that passion—and once more she was going to have to let it go. The difference was that she was older now. She no longer had the idealistic dreams of youth—imagining that what she felt for Alexei she might one day feel for another man. She wouldn't, and that was realism, not pessimism—and maybe life would be easier in a way, without the kind of passion which could carve you up into little pieces.

And she wasn't going to buckle under the burden of her heartache or the final shattering of her dreams—at least not in front of him.

'I really am turning you down,' she agreed calmly. She lifted her chin, like someone going into a room full of enemies, but her only enemy was the instinct which urged her to hurl herself into his arms and beg him to kiss her, to love her. She steeled herself against it. 'I'm going back to the Astronome. And tomorrow evening I'll fly home. As planned.'

There was a slow-motion fuzzy moment, when he could have stopped her, but the moment that followed told him he would be a fool to try. The world changed back into sharp real-time.

'Very well,' said Alexei, his voice as cold as ice. 'I will have someone arrange your flight back to London.'

CHAPTER TEN

FROM his office on the twenty-ninth floor of the Christou headquarters Alexei stared out at the cloudless blue sky and scowled. His black eyes followed the movement of an aeroplane which became a small silver dot as it travelled soundlessly away to an unknown future.

He hadn't slept a wink last night. Maybe he'd grown used to having the warm, slim shape of Victoria wrapped in his arms—and their last conversation had been buzzing round and round inside his head.

At least today she would be flying home. Soon she would be gone—back to England where she belonged—and he could get on with his life again.

He turned around to see the dark coffee cooling on his desk, and next to the newspapers a small bronze statue of a nymph, which had been a gift from his grandfather.

But no photos.

His desk was not like those of his counterparts. There was no close-up of a wife. No smiling portraits of cute children—or any of their clumsily executed but lovingly framed crayon drawings. His leather diary was studded with prestigious invitations—the possibilities endless.

So why did it suddenly feel so empty?

And why did he suddenly feel so alone?

Because he was, that was why. He had all the wealth and prestige in the world and he was isolated by them. Alone in his gilded tower.

Had his new wife felt like this when she had first come out here? Victoria had been forced to accept the situation he had put her in with no means of escape. And when it had become too much she had run to the only place she'd known. Her own home. Where a completely different set of social rules had existed. Where young women *did* share flats with men, without necessarily having sex with them. He had fallen in love and married a girl from that world, and yet he'd despised her for refusing to let go of it.

For the first time he recognised that he had not helped her to settle in Greece—he had just dumped her and let her get on with it. In his arrogance hadn't he almost expected her to put up with *anything*— just because he had done her the honour of marrying her?

So was he going to let her run away again?

He picked up the phone and spoke rapidly in Greek. Eventually there was a click and he heard her soft voice.

'Victoria?'

Her voice was flat. 'Hello, Alexei.'

'Will you meet me for lunch?'

There was a pause. 'Why?'

'We didn't finish our conversation.'

'But there's nothing left to say on the subject.'

'Then let's change the subject. Talk about something new.'

Victoria gave a tired laugh. 'And what's that supposed to mean?'

He closed his eyes. 'I don't want you to go like this.' *In fact, I don't want you to go at all.*

Victoria flopped down onto one of the brocade sofas and stared up at the chandelier. So he wanted a civilised goodbye? She glanced at her watch. There were seven long hours to kill before she caught her flight to London—what else was she going to do? Sit here telling herself that she wasn't going to cry? Or go out there and show the world—and, more importantly, *him*—that she was going to survive perfectly well?

'Where are you taking me?' she questioned flippantly.

Alexei was unprepared for the sudden stirring of hope. 'I will take you to the very best restaurant in Athens,' he promised unevenly. 'And send a car for you.'

'No, you won't,' said Victoria quietly, because this was the beginning of her new life, post-Alexei, and she was going to have to start behaving like lesser mortals again. The days of chauffeur-driven cars and luxury suites and private jets were over. But none of that seemed to matter. She was dreading going back, but the great gap in her life wasn't going to be the missing luxuries—but missing the man she had married.

'I'll get a taxi,' she said. 'What's the name of the restaurant?'

'Why are you so damned stubborn?' he murmured. 'It's close to the office. Have you a pen?'

The hotel staff had warned her about the lunchtime traffic, and so Victoria left plenty of time to get there. Too much time, in fact—because she arrived with a clear half-hour to spare.

The taxi driver glanced over his shoulder as she paid him, and she stepped outside into the blistering heat. So, she could go inside and wait with a cool drink.

Or…

The Christou building was just at the end of the block—wouldn't it be better to go there and surprise Alexei, rather than sit alone in a restaurant she didn't know?

She began walking towards the skyscraper—but it was a bit like being hurled into the centre of a kiln, and enough to make tiny beads of sweat prickle on Victoria's forehead.

The air-conditioning of the foyer hit her with a

welcome cold blast, and she smoothed the hair off her hot cheeks to realise that she was being watched closely by the same brunette who'd been on Reception the day she'd arrived.

The woman was looking no more friendly now than she had then. If anything, she looked worse. Alexei ought to do himself a favour and employ someone who looked as though they actually enjoyed working there, Victoria thought. And while he was at it perhaps he could choose someone who didn't look like as if she'd stepped straight from the pages of a glossy magazine!

Her bare legs felt sticky as she walked towards the desk, while the receptionist looked as cool as an ice-cube as she arched her perfectly plucked brows. 'Yes?' she said, without smiling. 'Can I help you?'

'Kalimera sas,' said Victoria politely. 'I'd like to see Kyrios Christou.'

'Do you have an appointment?'

Victoria frowned. Did the woman have a defective memory? Hadn't they had a similar conversation just last week? 'If it's all the same to you,' she said quietly, 'I don't think I actually *need* an appointment to see my husband!'

There was a pause. 'But you are getting divorced.'

'Excuse me?'

This time the brunette didn't miss a beat. 'You

are getting divorced, aren't you, Kyria Christou?' she repeated. 'So he isn't really your husband, is he?'

Victoria was so taken aback that for a moment she couldn't speak. But only for a moment. 'How... how dare you speak to me in that way?'

'But it is the truth, isn't it?'

Victoria hesitated, then drew herself up short. Why was she even *having* this conversation with a receptionist on Alexei's payroll? 'It's none of your business,' she said.

'I think it is.' The brunette met Victoria's stare with a flash of malice in her eyes. 'You see—we've been having an affair.'

Victoria laughed. 'In your dreams!'

'We've been lovers for six months now.'

It was one of those moments where the world spun and you thought you were in the middle of a terrible nightmare and prayed you might wake up. Until you realised you weren't going to.

Victoria's hands gripped the edge of the reception desk to steady herself.

'I don't believe you,' she breathed hoarsely.

'Well, you should.' The brunette flapped her eyelashes, but even their natural lushness couldn't disguise the poisonous glint in her eyes. 'Why would I lie to you? That day when you rang—remember?—I was on my knees in front of him, pleasuring him as he loves to be pleasured. Did he tell you that?'

Victoria's vision began to blur. 'No,' she moaned, then clamped her hand over her mouth—afraid that she might actually throw up.

'Yes. You were asking him for a divorce and he said he didn't want one. Surely you must have noticed that he sounded...' she gave a smug smile and chose exactly the right word in her sickeningly perfect English '...distracted?'

Victoria wanted to whimper, like an animal which had been wounded and left to die, and then to beat her fists in rage upon the shiny marble reception desk. But the woman was watching her closely— probably for just that reaction—and the maintenance of her pride suddenly seemed the most important thing in the world.

Biting back the meaningless words, she turned round and walked out of the building with her head held high, praying that her composure wouldn't crumple—and she managed it, until she hit the solid wall of heat outside.

Tears streaming down her face, she started to run until she could run no more in the impractical high-heeled sandals she had worn to impress the man who could still set her senses on fire. The man she had thought she was still in love with—and what on earth did that say about her judgement? That she could love such a heartless and faithless *bastard*?

Maybe she had the brunette to thank, for helping her see sense.

Somehow she found a cab to take her back to the Astronome, knowing that she had to get away from a place where all her judgement was shot to pieces. All she needed was her passport. The few clothes which were rightfully hers were now tainted with unbearable memories, and she couldn't even bear to *touch* the ones that Alexei had bought her.

It took nerve to walk down past the main desk without paying. She wanted to tell them that Alexei would settle the bill, but she didn't dare. For one thing she was afraid that she might burst into noisy sobs, and for another…what if they insisted on telephoning him to check, and he came tearing over here? She couldn't bear it.

And she had only herself to blame. Had she really thought that he was going to start treating her with kid gloves when she had entered into such a humiliating agreement in the first place?

The drive to the airport seemed like the longest of her life, because she couldn't shake off the fear that Alexei would come after her. She was told that she could have a ticket on a London-bound flight due to depart in under the hour—though she didn't let out a sigh of relief until she was safely airborne and Athens grew smaller, the buildings like tiny building blocks.

But the relief only lasted a nano-second, and the journey gave her no satisfaction. She was glad to leave and yet she didn't want to go home. She didn't want to go anywhere—except back to the place where she'd been before she had walked into Reception. When she still had her pride intact.

Well, she had been a fool for the last time in her life.

I hate you for what you've done, Alexei Christou, she vowed. *But I hate myself more for having let you do it.* And then—because the man beside her had started snoring—Victoria gave in to what she had been wanting to do all afternoon.

And wept.

CHAPTER ELEVEN

ALEXEI'S face grew dark.

'What do you mean, she's left?' he thundered in Greek.

The reply was the same as it had been before. They were very sorry, but the Englishwoman had gone—and no message had been left for him.

'You are certain of this?' he demanded, aware that he was running the risk of making himself sound like a fool. But suddenly his reputation was the last thing he was thinking about.

'*Ne*, Kyrio Christou.'

Alexei turned away, trying to put his muddled thoughts into some semblance of order. But nothing helped. What the hell had happened?

He had rushed through his morning's work, having to force himself to concentrate on the matters in hand. For once it had been hard to stay focussed. His mind had kept drifting off—haunted by the images of Victoria which kept drifting into his mind to distract him. Even after he'd showered, her scent still seemed to cling to his skin. He could almost see the honeyed silk of her hair as it spread all over his bare chest, could almost feel her soft body beneath his, on top of his, around his...

But her sex appeal was nothing new. It was more than that. The way it always had been—something indefinable and precious about the way she made him feel. In a way she both sapped his strength and gave him strength. Sometimes, after loving, she cradled his head against her breast and stroked his tousled black hair with gentle fingers. A man could feel as if he'd come home at a moment like that.

His dark doubts of earlier had been melting away, leaving something fresh and hopeful in their wake. He had been planning to tell her that he'd been selfish in never looking at things from her point of view. He had been planning to use all his charm to persuade her to stay. Yet now they were telling him that she'd gone.

'She has taken everything?' he questioned.

'*Ochi*, Kyrios Christou.'

'She hasn't?' His heart leapt. That was it—there must be some kind of explanation. And even while logic told him that there *was* no explanation—other than the glaringly obvious one—his mind refused to believe it. He raced up the stairs to her suite, but as soon as he walked in he knew that something was very wrong.

His mouth dried as he swallowed down the bitter taste in his mouth.

Oh, yes, she had left some of her stuff there—some very particular stuff. Everything that he had bought for her, in fact. Every bra, dress, pair of panties and negligee. The string of black pearls and the diamond earrings. He picked up a discarded silk stocking and closed his eyes as he held it beneath his nostrils.

What the hell had gone wrong?

At that moment the general manager knocked on the door of the suite, and Alexei—his face growing darker by the second—listened to what he had to say.

'You saw her leave the building *in tears*?' he demanded of the man in disbelief. 'And yet you did not think to tell me?'

The man shrugged, not saying any more—not needing to. And even in the midst of his anger Alexei knew what he must be thinking. Even if it was the manager's place to do any such thing, Kyrios Christou had a reputation as a heartbreaker, and a woman's tears were probably nothing new.

And that much was true—for women always wept, no matter how much they had insisted they would be happy with what you were prepared to offer them.

What was the use of saying that it was different with Victoria—that she was the woman he'd married?

But she had given him no hint of any real distress when he had spoken to her on the phone. She had even sounded flippant and made him smile. Made him ache, too.

So what had happened in the meantime to cause her to cry and leave without a word?

Troubled inside, he was driven at speed back to the Christou headquarters, and as he walked into Reception he noticed the brunette whom he probably should have let go—if he hadn't been so tied up with work and thinking about Victoria.

Her eyes lit up with a voracious sexual hunger when she saw him—and with something else, too. Was it guilt or was it triumph—or a mixture of both?

Alexei frowned and shook his head, like a swimmer clearing his head after emerging from deep water, as everything slotted into its nightmare place. A nerve worked at his cheek.

'Alexei?'

'What did you say to her?' he hissed.

She affected ignorance. 'Who?'

'Do not *lie* to me! And do not treat me like an idiot!' he exploded. 'What did you say *to my wife*?'

'She was not your wife when I had you in my mouth!' she snapped.

Blood pounded in his ears. His world spun. 'Did you tell her that?' he questioned dangerously.

'Of course I did! Because it is the truth!'

His hands clamped into tight fists by the shafts of his legs, for if he'd thought his rage dark before— now it was simply murderous. 'Get out,' he said simply. 'And get out now.'

'You treat your women badly, don't you, Alexei?' she accused hotly.

'Professionally, you will be treated fairly.' His mouth curved with contempt. 'Personally, I treat women only as they allow themselves to be treated,' he scorned, but his heart was pounding as he made his way towards the elevator and up to his office suite.

Was it too late?

Very probably.

And for the first time in his life Alexei recognised that he might have taken one risk too far.

But he must go to her.

His assistant was waiting for him as the elevator doors opened. 'Prepare the plane,' Alexei snapped.

The time for tears was over.

When she was back at home, Victoria splashed her face with cold water and dried it, quite calm again now. Only her puffy eyes and red-tipped nose gave away the fact that she had been crying.

She had to face facts—painful as they were. She'd been left feeling heartbroken and betrayed—but she was going to get better. She was. She had recovered from the end of her marriage to Alexei once before—so surely a second time would be easier?

The most pressing point was that she had walked away without her settlement—but she was damned well going to make sure she got it. After all, she

had earned it! And she wasn't going to be cowed
by Alexei—not any more. She would send him an
e-mail and ask that he transfer to her bank the
money which was rightfully hers. She had sought
and found an inner strength to help her deal with
what had happened—but she didn't think she was
up to speaking to him. Not yet.

Maybe not ever.

There was a ring on the doorbell. That would be
Caroline 'tell me *everything*'. She had said she'd try
to call round after she'd been to the supermarket.
Victoria still hadn't decided to go with the whole
shocking story or to give her friend a watered-down
account of just how she'd been spending her time
in Athens.

She pulled open the door and swiftly tried to shut
it again when she saw it was Alexei, not Caroline,
who stood there—but he stuck his foot in the door
like an old-fashioned detective.

'Get out!'

'I am not going anywhere!'

'Well, I don't want to see you!' she snapped.
'That's why I left without saying goodbye. Can't
you get the message, Alexei?'

'You cannot just run away after what has happened!' he exploded.

'Oh, can't I? I can do what the hell I like! Just
like you can!' Her mouth curved with contempt.
'Except that I would never stoop quite *so low*.'

'Let me speak to you, Victoria,' he said, softening his deep voice to a tone she had never heard him use before. 'Please.'

'What is there to say that hasn't already been said?' she questioned, her heart racing with pain. 'Unless you want to start describing *all* your sexual shenanigans with your employees? Have you worked your way through the entire workforce?'

He knew that he was in no position to protest against such a ludicrous accusation. 'I will not leave here until you listen to me,' he vowed. 'Believe me when I tell you that.'

'Do what you want,' she said, walking over to the far side of the room and deliberately turning her back on him, her heart racing even more as she heard the soft click of the door closing.

She whirled round, but he was still there, silent and forbidding, as if he had been carved from some rich, dark stone. 'Just say what it is you want to say, and then go.'

'*Theos,*' he groaned, raking his hand through his thick, dark hair. 'I am sorry, Victoria.'

'Sorry you did it, or sorry I found out?' she demanded.

'What do you think?'

The ravaged look on his face momentarily fazed her, but she stonewalled the feeling. 'Did it make you feel good to be having an affair with two women at the same time?' she raged, but the broken feeling in her stupid, forgiving heart made her feel as though her body had been split in two. 'Or maybe it fed your ego? Though I'm surprised you felt a need to! I thought your ego was quite big enough!'

'I was *not* having an affair with her at the same time as you!'

'So she was lying about giving you oral sex while you were on the phone to me, was she?' She looked at his stricken face and actually thought that she might faint. She dug her nails into the palms of her hands. 'No, I thought not,' she said slowly, and the blood roared like the sound of the sea in her ears.

He wanted to shout, and to rail against his own arrogant stupidity—but he knew he must tread oh-so-carefully if he was ever going to be able to salvage this.

'For God's sake, Victoria—it had been seven years! We had not spoken in all that time! I'm not clairvoyant! I didn't live the life of a monk on the off-chance that you might ring me on a whim one day, asking me for a divorce!'

'Obviously not,' she snapped.

'And I was not sleeping with her when you arrived in Athens. I swear that to you, Victoria!'

'I didn't ask you to swear anything!'

'In fact,' he ground out, 'when you rang it destroyed all my desire for any woman other than you!'

She looked at him with disdain. 'And I'm supposed to be grateful for this, am I?'

'I am trying to tell you the truth,' he declared.

But Victoria had tasted hurt again, and couldn't bear any more of its bitterness. She forced herself to keep the chill in her voice. 'Well, you've had me now—so let's just put it down to experience, shall we? You've had the sex, but I still haven't had the rest of my money—so if you wouldn't mind I'd like my settlement, and then I'd like you to go.'

'Even though I love you?' he questioned slowly. But his heart sank, for her eyes showed no forgiveness, only anger.

'Don't you *dare* say that! Don't you *dare* misuse those words just to get your own arrogant way!'

'I say it because I mean it, and for no other reason!' he retorted, and prayed for the right words to show her that he did mean it. 'You have brought the colour back into my life—and the reason—and—' He smote the flat of his hand dramatically over his heart. 'And the passion,' he finished, his voice softening but his eyes taking on the determined glint that she knew so well.

'And you know something? I think that deep down you love me, too, Victoria. That you know this woman meant nothing to me, but she is a useful excuse—a let-out clause because you are scared.' He held his hands out in supplication. 'And I am scared, too, Victoria—for what we are contemplating is a giant step.'

She shook her head. 'No, Alexei,' she whispered. 'You can't get what it is you think you want just by admitting vulnerability.' But wasn't it that self-same vulnerability which had made her realise that she still loved him? And wasn't he right about the brunette? Victoria *had* made the phone call to him out of the blue. Had she really thought that this hot-blooded man would have been celibate all these years? 'Why didn't you refuse to take the call?' she demanded.

'Because my assistant put it straight through!'

She drew a deep breath—because all she had left was honesty. And maybe a little pride. 'I can't be your mistress. I can't settle for that, Alexei. Maybe if we hadn't been husband and wife I could have done—but it won't work.'

'You don't love me?' he challenged. 'Because if you tell me that I will not believe you, Victoria. Your lips may tell me one thing, but your eyes quite another.'

Take courage, she told herself on a deep breath. A person couldn't change the way they felt, no matter how much they wanted to—but they could change their behaviour. She could modify the way she reacted to her feelings, if she needed to protect herself. And she did. She needed all the help she could get.

'Yes, I love you. I can't seem to help myself loving you. But that doesn't mean that there's any future in it. All the fundamentals are still there, I agree. The chemistry, and the way we feel about each other—but the things which helped split us up are still there too. Why would anything be any different now?'

'Because we are older and in charge of our destiny!' he stormed, like a man pleading for his life before the executioner—and that was exactly how it felt. As if Victoria held the key to his future as well as his heart. 'We can make our own decision about how we live our lives—for I am no longer the apprentice. I run the company!'

'And you'll end up in an early grave, if you don't slow down!'

'Are you saying you think that I shouldn't work?'

'I wouldn't dream of advising you how to live your life,' she retorted, and then she saw a glimpse of real pain in his eyes—and the shock of that simply took her breath away. For he was hurting, too— just as she was. So was she going to continue punishing him? Punishing herself? 'Oh, Alexei,' she whispered.

He let out a ragged sigh, recognising in her voice the first faint glimmer of hope. But his whole life had been spent fighting and winning boardroom battles, and instinct told him that his prize was in no way assured.

'I wasn't expecting what happened to happen,' he said softly. 'I was not expecting to want you so much—and even when I did I thought that once would be enough. Or maybe twice. I thought that you were a hunger I could satisfy—but you were not, Victoria.' His eyes glittered like black stars. 'You still aren't. You never will be.'

'You cold-bloodedly made me your mistress because you knew that I needed the money!' she raged. 'It wasn't just about sex—it was all about revenge!'

'Yes, it was. But now it has changed, Victoria *mou*,' he said slowly. 'You know that and I know that. I was not expecting to feel *this* again…this *love* which makes everything else in the world seem so insignificant.'

Victoria wavered, but the pull of what she really wanted was too strong to resist. They could bat their anger around all afternoon, but surely there was only one thing that really mattered? And Victoria could hold out no longer. She let out a sigh which felt as if it had been sucked from her soul, and in it he seemed to sense a kind of surrender, for he held his arms open and she went into them—like a child seeking refuge from the storm.

He held her tightly to him, burying his face in the silken splendour of her hair, breathing in its sweet scent as if it were the very breath of life, shaken beyond measure by what he had had within his grasp and had come so close to losing.

'I do not deserve this,' he said at last.

'True,' she agreed shakily, but the tears were springing hot and salty to her eyes.

He drew away from her, his eyes darkening when he saw that hers were wet. He wiped each teardrop away with the tip of his finger, his expression alive with warmth and love. 'Will you be my wife?' he questioned tenderly.

'I thought I already was.'

'I meant…properly,' he said fiercely.

'And there was me hoping that you meant improperly… Oh…Alexei!' His name was muffled by the hard, seeking pressure of his kiss. She touched her fingertips to his olive cheek. 'But what about your mother? Won't she go mad when she finds out?'

Alexei gave a rueful smile. 'She once told me that the light went out in my eyes after we split up.'

'*Did* she?'

'She did. Mothers have the knack of speaking truthfully to their children.' His dark eyes narrowed. 'But then, she wants me to have children of my own.'

'And…do you?'

'I do,' he said unsteadily.

'Me, too,' she whispered shyly.

Alexei nodded and bit his lip—his emotions almost too raw to contain. 'But not yet.' He pulled her into his arms again, closing his eyes tightly shut, not wanting her to know how close to tears he was himself...he who had come so close to losing the most important thing in the world to him.

EPILOGUE

THE wind whipped at Victoria's hair as the sleek white lines of the *Aphrodite* cut through the sapphire waves like a knife through soft butter.

Victoria stood on the deck, breathing in the heady salt tang of the spray, and felt Alexei move up behind her, slipping his hands around her waist and nuzzling at her neck.

'It was a good weekend?' he murmured.

'Mmm.' She leaned back against his strong chest. 'A perfect weekend.' They had attended the wedding of Alexei's younger sister—a happy family occasion at the Christou family villa in Vouliagmeni. The house where she had spent those first ill-starred months of her marriage no longer held bitter memories—for they had been melted away by what she and Alexei had today.

'My mother adores you,' he said softly.

She knew that it was reassurance he was offering, but it was something she no longer needed. 'I know she does, darling Alexei—and I've grown to adore her, too.' She did not find the imposing matriarch intimidating any more, and both women were eager to compromise after what had happened in the past.

In the two years since they had renewed their wedding vows, Alexei's whole life had been transformed by the woman he had first made his wife so long ago. Maybe he'd had just had the ability to recognise a true gem at the time, he thought, with a flare of his customary arrogance.

Alexei looked out to sea, where he could the first faint curve of land breaking the stark blue line of the horizon. They were headed for his island—now *their* island—an exquisite spot where they could be truly alone. And those times were the most precious of all to him. For the lure of the boardroom and the big deal had faded. Life was there to be savoured, and she made that so easy.

'Happy?' he questioned softly, for she had appeared a little tired at lunch.

'Eftihismenos,' she agreed, in her increasingly fluent Greek—because this time she wasn't going to make the mistakes of the past. Neither of them were. Greek lessons were not a luxury, but a necessity—and she was mature enough now to see them as an intellectual challenge. It wasn't an easy language to learn—but it was a beautiful one. And she wanted to be able to understand her children…when she had them.

She found her face growing pink. She had only found out that morning, and had hugged the secret to herself, wanting to find the perfect moment to tell him.. and, in a day full of perfect moments, this one seemed as good as any.

Victoria stood on tiptoe to kiss his proud, beautiful mouth, waiting to drink in and capture his reaction as she prepared to tell him about the sweet product of their love.

'Alexei *mou*,' she said softly. 'I have something to tell you…'

A Special Offer from

HARLEQUIN Presents

This August, purchase 6 Harlequin Presents books and get these THREE books for FREE!

ONE NIGHT WITH THE TYCOON
by Lee Wilkinson

IN THE MILLIONAIRE'S POSSESSION
by Sara Craven

THE MILLIONAIRE'S MARRIAGE CLAIM
by Lindsay Armstrong

To receive your THREE FREE BOOKS, send us 6 (six) proofs of purchase from August Harlequin Presents books to the addresses below.

In the U.S.:	In Canada:
Presents Free Book Offer	Presents Free Book Offer
P.O. Box 9057	P.O. Box 622
Buffalo, NY	Fort Erie, ON
14269-9057	L2A 5X3

- -

Name (PLEASE PRINT)

Address   Apt. #

City   State/Prov.   Zip/Postal Code

098 KKJ DXJN

www.eHarlequin.com

HARLEQUIN *Presents*

She's in his bedroom, but he can't buy her love....

Showered with diamonds, draped in exquisite lingerie, whisked around the world...

The ultimate fantasy becomes a reality in Harlequin Presents!

When Nora Lang acquires some business information that top tycoon Blake Macleod can't risk being leaked, he must keep Nora in his sight.... He'll make love to her for the whole weekend!

MISTRESS FOR A WEEKEND
by Susan Napier

Book #2569,

on sale September 2006

www.eHarlequin.com

HPMTM0906

If you enjoyed what you just read,
then we've got an offer you can't resist!

Take 2 bestselling love stories FREE!

Plus get a FREE surprise gift!

Clip this page and mail it to Harlequin Reader Service®

IN U.S.A.
3010 Walden Ave.
P.O. Box 1867
Buffalo, N.Y. 14240-1867

IN CANADA
P.O. Box 609
Fort Erie, Ontario
L2A 5X3

YES! Please send me 2 free Harlequin Presents® novels and my free surprise gift. After receiving them, if I don't wish to receive anymore, I can return the shipping statement marked cancel. If I don't cancel, I will receive 6 brand-new novels every month, before they're available in stores! In the U.S.A., bill me at the bargain price of $3.80 plus 25¢ shipping & handling per book and applicable sales tax, if any*. In Canada, bill me at the bargain price of $4.47 plus 25¢ shipping & handling per book and applicable taxes**. That's the complete price and a savings of at least 10% off the cover prices—what a great deal! I understand that accepting the 2 free books and gift places me under no obligation ever to buy any books. I can always return a shipment and cancel at any time. Even if I never buy another book from Harlequin, the 2 free books and gift are mine to keep forever.

106 HDN DZ7Y
306 HDN DZ7Z

Name	(PLEASE PRINT)	
Address	Apt.#	
City	State/Prov.	Zip/Postal Code

Not valid to current Harlequin Presents® subscribers.

Want to try two free books from another series?
Call 1-800-873-8635 or visit www.morefreebooks.com.

* Terms and prices subject to change without notice. Sales tax applicable in N.Y.
** Canadian residents will be charged applicable provincial taxes and GST.
All orders subject to approval. Offer limited to one per household.
® are registered trademarks owned and used by the trademark owner or its licensee.

PRES04R
©2004 Harlequin Enterprises Limited

Dinner at 8...
Don't be late!

He's suave and sophisticated,
He's undeniably charming.
And above all, he treats her like a lady.

But don't be fooled....

Beneath the tux, there's a primal passionate
lover, who's determined to make her his!

Wined, dined and swept away by a British billionaire!